The Deaf Boy Who Could

DANCE

SUE LAURA

authorHOUSE®

AuthorHouse™ UK Ltd.
500 Avebury Boulevard
Central Milton Keynes, MK9 2BE
www.authorhouse.co.uk
Phone: 08001974150

First published by AuthorHouse 1/10/2011

ISBN: 978-1-4567-7148-5 (sc)

www.suelaura.webs.com

This book is printed on acid-free paper.

BIT ABOUT THE AUTHOR

Sue Laura was born in 1969 in South London. Although she didn't like school very much she always had a hankering to write a book. She is a working mum to three boys and has very strong family values.

MY DEDICATIONS

My Boys. Daniel, Antony and Terry – You three are all that matters in my life. You give me strength and reasons to go on and on.

Terry & Barbara Harmer. – My loving parents. Without your love and support throughout my whole life I would not be here today nor the person I am. Thank you for everything.

George Pavlou – Forever I will hold you in my heart. Rest in peace darling.

Christians dedication page

Riannah – *I never knew you but I can remember you. Thank you for giving me your grace and emotions. Rest in peace my true mother.*

Luis – *Always a treasure to me. My brother I love you.*

Jay – *Thank you for your inspiration, drive patient and push. A true friend whom I will never forget*

Jo - *You were always my Jo*

The Deaf Society – *Never give up on your hopes and dreams. You can feel the music deep inside, its there just search for it.*

The Gay Society – *B – GAP!*

And finally

Sasha – *The girl in my life.*

Thank you

Big Sis – For believing in my dreams

CONTENTS

1.   My Home And Me 1
2.   Meet The Family 13
3.   Saskia 25
4.   Discovery 31
5.   Dancing 35
6.   Jay 51
7.   Saskia A Mum 61
8.   That Man 69
9.   The Miracle Of Sound 91
10. Good Times Turn 97
11. The Father 111
12. Gio 119
13. Family Business 125
14. Niko's Death 131
15. Laid To Rest 141
16. UK 153
17. Kelso 167
18. New York City 177
19. My Girl 187
20. Jeanne 195
21. Jesee 203
22. Life Updated 217
Epilog 225

CHAPTER 1

MY HOME AND ME

Corfu stands at the entrance of the Adriatic Sea. It straddles the Albanian and Greek frontiers and is barely 50 miles from the heel of Italy.

Romans, Germans, Turkish, French, Russians, Italians and British - Corfu has seen them all and taken a little from each in becoming the proud and exciting island it is today.

Corfu has its own island character….. It lies in a rippling turquoise sea. Clear as glass revealing the wide variety of marine life below. With its unique position contributing to the tempestuous history of this greenest of Greek islands, Corfu boasts beautiful scenery due to its green and abundant foliage. The endless groves of silvery olive trees, lovely beaches and luxuriant vegetation coupled with the sound of the sea and the songs of a thousand birds, this paradise is locally known as the

Emerald Island. To wake up each morning to the beautiful and catching scenery is a joy to behold and where else on earth would I rather be? The future holds a lot of intrigue for me and many people I will meet on my travels. But before I begin my story let me give you an insight on what it was like to grow up in Corfu and the lives of the people I mixed with.

Corfiots are charming, endearing people who retain a fresh, open and simplistic approach to life. To an observer Corfiots appear casual, their pace of life seems unhurried but it is not always the case however! Impatience also exists and will be demonstrated at bus stops, shop counters and in banks where only visitors would dream of queuing up quietly!

The people of Corfu take their Orthodox religion, with its elaborate ceremonies, most seriously. It is a common sight to see the black robed priests with their long beards bustling through the streets all around the island. Perhaps the most marvellous thing about Corfu would be that it has absorbed so much of its past and yet has changed so little. Peasant women still jog along side-saddle on their mules carrying home bundles of firewood. When you gaze at the fishing nets draped across the quays in the sunset, as they always have, one feels that the beauty of this island will endure, as it has to date.

Scattered on this island paradise lay numerous villages and small towns, daily buzzing with the hustle and bustle of life, mules braying as they carry their heavy loads, worn out by the heat of the noonday sun. One of these small villages was the home of my family. We did not appear to be anything out of the ordinary, just a normal every day family. The houses were traditionally Greek and would be large but continually built on as a family grew, and also to make space for extended members of the family. Our house was this way; there was always plenty of room for me to run and play and to sometimes hide when I needed my privacy.

Our home nestled on the hillside amongst the olive groves. A small village with cobbled streets and whitewashed buildings, with hanging baskets full of beautiful rich colours of the flowers contained in them. Located in an orchard of almond trees, a lemon tree, vines and mulberry trees was our family home. To the front of the house lay a secluded lawn with a private patio furnishing two gas-fired barbecues, a griddle and spit roast, to cook the wonderful aromatic meats that only Mama knew how.

It was a two-storey, clean and comfortable home. White washed walls outside with a beautiful red roof glinting in the brilliant sunshine. Inside was as lavish as Mama could afford at the time. A vast space, although from the outside it looked quite small. The floors all lay in wood with large terracotta rugs, they were always crisp and clean. Mama was a bit of a freak with her cleanliness so everywhere was always gleaming and spotless. Even the light shades she cleaned every week. The colours of the furnishings were outstanding but all looked immaculate and co-ordinated. The heavy cream coloured curtains to keep the cold night air out, hung in pools on the floor. In the middle of the lounge sat a beautiful wooden table, sometimes my friends would put their feet on it to be comfortable. Mama always made my friends feel at home, but when she saw them with their feet on the table she came along with her feather duster and quickly but firmly brushed their feet off. "Not in MY house you not" she would say in her typically Greek tongue.

To go to the upstairs one had to negotiate a winding marble staircase, but once you got to the top Oh my word! What a haven of decadence! The bedrooms all decorated to the taste of the occupant. My bedroom was my private haven and I was very proud and happy to be able to arrange it as I wished. The floors marbled as downstairs but there was a rug on the floor by my bed so as not to step out of my warm bed and straight onto a cold floor. My bed was so comfortable and my nights spent in it were warm and cosy. The window was quite small but nevertheless I had superb views from it. Being next door to Mamas room I too was afforded the view of the rushing waves and cliffs. I had a wardrobe which housed my clothes and an old chest of drawers next to it. On top of the chest of drawers I had my favourite pictures of my family. The curtains were dark as a child to blacken the room so I could sleep when the daylight shone into my room it made shadows on the wall from the glinting of my trophies.

The house had a sea view from the balcony in Mama's room to the left of the door. The view to the south side seemed to hang right over the waves, with a glorious sweep of cliff, sea and mountains dominating the view, whilst the west facing rooms looked directly across to the old vine terraces and pine woods. The house was surrounded by a cluster of traditional fishing cottages, tavernas, village shops with the harbour nestling beneath the caves, cliffs and old vine terraces of the headland. There is a beach here, and even on those afternoons when the wind sets the surf pounding against the rocks, also dolphins, and on rare occasion's even turtles, could sometimes be seen in the surrounding sea.

Many times I would sneak into Mama's room and gaze longingly across the Ionian Sea and wonder if there ever would be a future for me out there. I loved my home and my family very much, but would often think that there was certainly something out there for me. This was when I had a surge of the inquisitive to go and search for my dream of becoming someone important and that I could make Mama proud of me. She had been through a lot for me as I was born deaf, and as anyone knows who has been through it, to try and communicate with a deaf child is not an easy thing to do.

The land our house stood on was situated in a walled garden with several ponds and lakes, where from the time we were very young my brothers and sister and myself learnt to swim. Many times our friends would come and we would play water games in the pool creating all manner of havoc in the walled garden coming and going throughout the summer months. Mama would throw us straight in and we either learnt to swim or we sank. The fun we had was amazing and we became very close as a family with our friends.

My friends respected Mama and loved her very much. She was always one to sit down with them and talk about their problems and to have fun with. She was very much respected with whomever she came into contact.

Adorning the large main wall in the lounge was a painting of Archbishop Makarios; Mama was very religious and took pride in the fact that she had a rather large picture of him on her wall. There were silky cushions scattered all over and on the floor sat some rather large bean bags for those who did not have a seat when they visited. You could only fit a couple of large sofas in the lounge so the additional seating provided was used when the family came over or Mama had one of her "social" evenings. People always visited Mama so she made sure that all were comfortable and well looked after when they visited. She was an excellent cook providing all manner of foods for ALL to enjoy. It was the custom in Corfu that when you visited people there would always be food and wine and excellent company and Mama was no different, in fact she excelled at whatever she did and that I believe is where I inherited my determination from. I never felt as at home as I did in that house, in the town where I grew up on that island; and I probably never will.

CHRISTIAN

I was born deaf. They told me I could say some words, or rather make verbal sounds, but I was typically very quiet. I listened with my eyes and always watched mouth and hand movements.

They said I had a cheeky boyish face with an appearance of innocence, a charming young guy with manners and warmth for everyone. I was always smiling, occasionally a full smile but most of the time a grinning half smile, at least that was what my family called it. As a very small child I would follow Mama everywhere, hanging onto her apron strings. When she cooked I would sit to the table with my crayons and pencils making all manner of pictures. I loved books especially the ones with pictures in. It was hard to read as being deaf I couldn't hear the pronunciation of the words and would get frustrated at not being able to understand. Mama did her best and looking back now she had the patience of a saint. My family tell me I was eager to learn but was frustrated because I couldn't learn quickly enough and would get angry. Many times I would sneak out and "borrow" one of my brothers' remote control toys and dismantle them and try and put them back together, but as I am sure you know once you take something apart it is rare that you get it back together in one piece with nothing left over. This caused a lot of problems between us but they didn't play with them anyway so what was their problem? By the age of eleven I had demolished quite a few things in trying to find out how they worked. I often sat and watched the television and wondered if there really were tiny people inside it. It wasn't until I eventually wrecked one of them that I realised my fantasy was not a reality. Of course I tried to put these things back together but as I am sure you all know you can never get ALL of the parts back in the right places and usually had bit and pieces left over. I guess these were the silly thoughts of a child, but I was left alone to explore my world. I was reprimanded when I had done something wrong but was never physically disciplined, it was always verbal and in some sort of sign language that Mama had learnt to enable contact between us all.

Family life was not extravagant and my clothes were always "hand me downs". This was not my idea of fun and inside me there was a person forming who needed to find their own way in the world. As I got older I developed a great liking for denim. I had some sort of fashion sense and back then hair styles were changing and I decided to change with them. Sometimes I would grow it long and have it in a pony tail hanging down my back, and sometimes I greased it back with gel which did, I have to admit, give me a sexier appeal than normal. Other times I would leave it loose to fly in the wind. Throughout the summer I could mostly be seen wearing a bandana to keep it off my face, as the weather was pretty hot and hair flying around your face when you are hot is not a good thing. Atop my head would always be my trade mark, big dark sunglasses. As I got older I cut my hair depending on my mood. I was a lazy shaver and most days would wear a partially unshaved goatee, but I think it added that bit of extra excitement to my look, and I have to say made me look sexier. Vanity! What a great fucking thing!

SCHOOL

School started off reasonably well but after a time it became a living nightmare. The only lesson I really enjoyed was physical education which enabled me to take part in many sports and activities. It was during these lessons that I became as good, if not better, than everyone else. I seemed to excel in every physical activity I took part in, mostly swimming, football and gymnastics.

I wasn't one for written work as I usually sat at the back of the class and felt left out of the lessons because of my hearing. You would think that I would be at the front of the class to lip read my teachers, but no, I had to sit at the back, and the teachers weren't very patient with me so I dropped behind everyone else. It seemed to me that the teachers just weren't bothered with helping me learn, it was too much like hard work for them to take the time and sit with me to explain, and none of the teachers could use sign language which made it even harder for them and me. I just used to sit by the window and stare out all day at the beach and I felt as if it was calling me. Recess times were a nightmare as I was picked on as a small child and called "thick" and "idiot". It was in the playground that I learnt to stand up for myself. My brothers, Riki and TJ had taught me how to hold my own and many a time they would back me up when one or more of the boys at school tormented me and it invariably ended up in a fight. My brothers and I fast became a force to be reckoned with both in school and in the neighbourhood. At times Teresa would even put her six penny worth in, especially where the girls were concerned. Coming from a tight knit family of three brothers she learnt to stand on her own two feet and with me being her baby brother she always had my back.

Reaching the age of 13 I made a decision that school was not for me. It became well known by my teachers and Mama that school was just hindering my progression in life. I didn't know where the rules on truancy from school stood but obviously Mama had got it sorted because, from that decision I had made nobody ever forced me to go to school again. As I learnt to speak the words became easier and my hunger to learn grew more intense. I used to read books at home but in a whisper as I was so ashamed of my voice because people used to laugh at the guttural sounds I made. I secretly wished to be able to speak the same as others, but the children at school were very cruel. They would mock my speech and the pitch of my voice and started calling me a "poofta" I wondered what this word meant so I looked it up in the dictionary and it meant "feminine, gay or very camp" in Greek. Kids would call me names like that because of the way in which I spoke and I would end up in fights to protect myself. When their parents found out what was happening at school and they learnt that I was deaf they made their children apologise to me, seeming very sincere and pretending to be sorry but they still picked on me at school. All the while they laughed at me and my family but I was going to show them. I didn't know how yet but I was going to show them that I was a person just the same as they and a much better person at that. Riki and TJ taught me how to fight and soon the kids in the playground knew they couldn't get away with calling me names and ridiculing my family. I could take care of myself and I was going to show them I was more important than them.

Mama was the one person in my life I could depend on and she helped me to learn the lessons I need to know. She taught me all the practicalities of life and how to take care of myself, as I am sure she knew that one day I would fly the nest and make it in the big wide world away from the village and people I had known all my life. To me and Mama these were the real lessons in life, how to care for myself from day to day, housework, washing and ironing and even change a light bulb and plug. These things were more important to me than learning about war and things that had gone in the past. Mama and I had a very close relationship and thinking back now as I write I am taken to my early teenage years, you know, the ones where a teenager knows everything and is living in that "I could die!" stage. Mama would openly cuddle and kiss us even when we didn't want it, especially in public. Mama was always proud of all of us and didn't mind making a fuss over us in front of others. Oh Mama!

It really is quite an insular world for a deaf person, if you want to be part of society you have to be bigger and better than a hearing person. This was a goal in my life to always be bigger and better than most others. There were very few people who had patience with a deaf person and I felt for a while as if I was intruding in their lives. It wasn't until a few years later when I reversed the situation and realised that hearing people are honoured to be part of MY world.

I loved to walk through the country side of home and just kick back on the beach and relax and take the beauty all in. I loved to swim and not just in the sea but in the little coves and bays. There was always one spot on the beach where I liked to go – you who know me truly know that spot. It was safe – a word you will often hear me refer to through this whole book. I fear life sometimes. People mocking my speech and "safe" people protected me. Safe to me is the best word I can think of to describe the warm feeling I get when I am with my loved ones, the people I trust. Safe means to me that I am protected, that the people who care for me are always there to help to give me confidence to stand up for myself. People I consider safe will hear me use it many times in conversation. Mama was the safest person to be with I knew she would never hurt me. Sometimes people I trusted would hurt me and I started to shy away from them for fear they would hurt me again. But Mama was always there, she was my security blanket. I knew I could depend on her.

CHAPTER 2

MEET THE FAMILY

Please let me introduce you to my family and the people I lived with for my formative years.

MAMA

Mama was my goddess, my idol, my sanctuary. She was born of Greek descent on the island of Cyprus. She had an arranged marriage to Toni and moved to Greece to start a new life and business. They had been together many years from when they were children. Mama worked hard for the house she had and for the finer things in life and so did Toni, for a while. You may notice I call Mama, Mama and I call him Toni – never really did like that man at all since I was a small kid but that's another chapter which I'll pursue later .

For as long as I can remember, she was there and I was holding on to her apron strings. She had other children to bring up, but I think being disabled made her more protective over me.

She was a tall woman – about five foot nine inches tall and built very sturdy. Her hair was shoulder length; black with streaks of gray running through it like forks of lightning, but it seemed to get shorter as the years went on! She had big, dark brown eyes with laughter lines running underneath them. Her skin olive and wrinkled from her exposure to the sun all her life, although she did not look haggard like most of the elderly women walking the cobbles. She always was smiling, laughing, and talking aloud. She would never be too quiet about things and sometimes would become carried away with explanations. She was never scared to give her opinion either and even though life had given her many challenges, she was always ready to help others in their adversities. She was considered by many to be rather loud, as she was always joking and the life of the party. She was the matriarch of our family and a deeply religious woman. Mama's dress and her actions would reflect her personality; she loved life and people. She would wear black tights always with a floral dress, and black soft slip-on shoes. Although traditionally religious she was also full of life, she smoked, drank wine and gave much love to all who met her. Although I couldn't hear in the early days I knew she was always singing, even when doing the mundane things of life like keeping the house clean. When she went to church on a Sunday, she would wear a matching pretty shawl over her dress and looked very fine, bringing it up over her head, as she would venture into the Church. My brothers and sister were not much into going to church either so I used to be the one to go every Sunday– YES EVERY

FUCKING PISSING SUNDAY – who would accompany her to Church holding her by the arm. She would parade around the others from the village like a fine tall peahen. She was a character. I couldn't sing anything in church but Mama was making enough noise for the both of us!!

I have many wonderful memories of that woman and her loving ways. On my 14th birthday, I watched her bake me a huge big creamy chocolate birthday cake. She was an artist in the kitchen and could create the most amazing tastes. That cake was the loveliest taste, which I will never ever forget. She always made my birthday's fun with lots of nice presents, a cake and friends over, music would play, and as we got older, we could smoke too. Mama, she smoked like a trooper and she could swear like a trooper too – if there were a gold medal in the Olympics for swearing – mama would have won it! Toni was actually a bastard to her really. That is how men here treated their women; well the older traditional ones did anyway. They treated their wives like shit and I hated this but she was a hard faced strong woman too who could certainly hold her own. Many a time I would get a clip around the head for swearing at the dinner table, or laughing aloud when someone else had been clipped too. Those were the days!

Market days would be so funny too, with Mama on my arm. I would walk with her to the market and wait outside every shop she went in and carried all of her bags. She stopped to chat to nearly everybody and it was normally always the same thing every other conversation!

When it came to shopping and walking around the village, you just knew Mama wanted to share all the news about what had been happening in and around the house with all us kids. She was a proud woman who loved to brag about us all. You could see it on her face when we stopped to talk to all the old crones – she would be patting me on my face and squeezing my face – making my hair pretty! She was too funny at times.

I do remember one of the funniest times was when she had been watching something on the television and it must have played on her mind as she didn't really know what she was talking about!!! She was talking to one of her oldest friends from church – we had bumped in to her coming back from shopping and Mama couldn't resist in telling her about things called BUTT PLUGS!!!!! OH MY GOD I NEARLY FELL ON THE FLOOR – **WHO'S MOTHER DOES THAT!??**

She certainly was a good willed person who loved to have a laugh too. Her youth shined through sometimes and even more so when that arsehole Toni was not around. She would always let others come over for dinner and stay overnight. She didn't like Saskia very much – infact she detested Saskia. Nevertheless, Saskia was like a piece of the furniture being at my house as much as she was. Mamas' health was not so good but she would go from day to day doing what she had to and what she was physically able. She was a martyr.

TONI

Where does one begin to describe a man like Toni? He was a taller man, say about six feet two inches but with a kind of a stoop in his back. He had pushed back hair kept in place by Bryl cream and it was salt and peppery kind of colour. His eyes were dark brown, almost black when he was in a rage. He had a big nose too and he wore glasses. Born in Cyprus Toni met Mama when she was young and they eloped to Corfu and started a life together. He was a lay about really, worked in the harbour most of his life, trawling for fish. That is probably why he always stunk to high heaven too. He would come and go really and was always out in the tavernas over the weekends drinking Ouzo with his mates and playing dominoes or cards. He gave Mama little really especially with four growing kids to raise and feed. He was spiteful to Mama and pushed her around quite a bit. We hated the way he treated her. However, it was not our place to tell him what to do in his own home. As we grew older, we would receive a backhander for answering back and told to shut up. We always had to watch our step and it was like walking on eggshells most of the time. I always knew he didn't like me and I could not work it out for a long time. He treated me so differently to the others, I hated it, and I hated him for it. I swore that when I grew and I became a man I would send him on his way so he could not hurt Mama again. As we grew older; if we were lucky, he would have invited us after dinner, to sit and smoke with him. I did not care for this and would just help Mama with Teresa cleaning dishes and tidying the kitchen area up. He never played cars with me, read me any books, or even learnt how to sign with me when I was learning and growing up; so I guess I didn't give a toss about him really. Mama was my parent. He so wanted to be the one who ran the house but Mama had routine and everything was orderly. He demanded respect; but to be honest he never got any, maybe if he had given respect to Mama we may have felt differently but hitting a woman!!!!? Only a coward does that! He was a loser and a ponce.

He may have worked hard in his line of business but it was not always for the family, but for the hired whores and the nights, he spent drinking and gambling. As a result he lost all the respect he had to start with and that was not much. We all knew he was shit but Mama wouldn't kick him out because of her religion. She felt she had to stick through it and not give up. She always felt there was some good in him deep down. I remember the first time he hit Mama, I was aged about seven and ever since then just the sight of this bully stuck in my throat. One day something would happen and he would not be in our lives any more.

Toni was not the father I had always imagined one to be. I wanted a father who would be proud of me in whatever I did. One who when I had performed would take me in his arms and hug me and say, "Well done son!" I would help him clean his car and visit him at his work. I would watch Toni with his sons, Riki and TJ and be a little jealous that I did not have what they had. It hurt very much but I learnt to live with the pain. Maybe there is some connection to wanting a father and having relationships with older men. I imagined my father as being someone in his thirties, good looking and full of energy. Maybe one day I would find my real father and he would be everything I hoped he would be.

RIKI

Riki was Mamas first born. Of dark hair, brown eyes, an olive skin and a clear complexion he was a very handsome young man, but as he grew older he had to wear glasses. He stood a tall six feet. He was Mama's model child really from baby to young man. He went to school all the time and attended Greek school at weekends without missing a day. He did his homework on time and always completed his house chores. He never smoked or even tried smoking as far as I know. Riki did not hug or kiss anyone in the family unless he had to. He was not a "hands on, and show your emotions" person. He never showed any interest in dating until he left school and went to college. He was studying to be an accountant. He was already keeping books for a couple of local businesses so he really was doing well. It was not long before he graduated with qualifications under his belt, and, from there he went on to work for a known accountant as part of a team. He met the girl (a typical Greek girl her name – Helena – meaning light) who he then went on to marry. The wedding was a traditional Greek affair. Riki was always the sensible one. He always had time for me and was always a good person. I always had time for him too but he was a bit older than me so we did not really hang out together like TJ and I did He had a very good relationship with Mama. He respected Toni too. He was their first-born and he made them proud. He was a good brother too.

Riki had an almost "Mr Bean" type of character. When he danced, he was very stiff in his upper body and he had lanky legs with long arms but he smiled which made him look quite funny. He liked traditional Greek dance and we often took to the floor together when Mama used to show us off. That was the only time I really had physical contact with my older brother. I could imagine he would go on to become very well educated and a highly paid man in whatever field he chose. I could see him with the traditional Greek wedding and a traditional Greek wife. He was a home bird and would do all the traditional things we Greeks had been raised to live and believe. When his family was coming along, he would hand down the "old ways" to his children and so it goes on throughout history, generation to generation the morals and values we were taught as children. Riki was passionate about his hometown. He supported the local team A O Kerkyra, he used to go and watch them with Toni when he was around. Riki was a talking type of man not a fighter, he believed that no disagreements would be settled with violence and hated it. He could take care of himself though and would stand up for any one he cared for. Nevertheless, he had a quiet respect about him that people softened and listened to him. He was a gentle man and everyone loved him. You would never hear him argue with Mama, and in our house it was she who metered out the discipline. I guess he was quicker than the rest of us in knowing it wasn't a good idea to go against Mama. He always had patience with TJ and TJ in turn looked up to him with much respect. He took care of Teresa, and looked out for all of us as by this time Toni was hardly ever around, and had no backbone anyway. He never touched smoke or anything stronger than paracetamol for a headache. He really was the cream of the family. He was forever saying "bastadio!" to TJ and I whenever we lit up a smoke and he was around. Toni tried to get Riki into smoking but he was having none of it.

TJ

TJ stood for Toni junior. He was the baby of Mama's family, just a year older than me. I think TJ and I were actually were very close until our teenage years. He was all of 5 foot 10 inches tall with light brown hair. He was less Greek looking than Riki. He tolerated school and went all the time he had to, but he didn't want to stay on for further education. He left school at 16 to go and work in a nearby restaurant, cooking. He smoked cigarettes; infact, TJ smoked everything he could, including cigars and tea bags. DON'T ASK! He liked a drink too but certainly couldn't handle it. He would get drunk so much he would throw up for hours! He learned to use sign language too so we could talk more and that was fun at times. We used to roam a lot when we were about 12 or 13. We would climb trees, swim in the bays, played volleyball and footie. He would come down to the den at times when we was about 14 or 15 and we would smoke cigarettes and have drinks together till we got wrecked and we would giggle like mad! Often, on those nights, he would tell me how he so wanted to have Saskia, I never wanted to hear it but I always listened. We would end up fighting a lot – I mean it's alright for other boys from the village, but not us especially as we were brothers! They had heard we had quite a hard reputation so they were always offering us out. We were the hardest though and always won our scraps. No one fucked with our Mama, or our sister Teresa and any of us. He was often in trouble for not doing his schoolwork and often received a clip round the head for swearing or not doing his chores! Toni used to give him a cigarette at times and they would sit and spend quality time talking and smoking together. He called Riki a prick most of the time and didn't have a lot of time for Teresa unless her girlfriends were over! TJ was great looking and he knew it! He was always roaming for girls or perving. He was always talking about leaving home and having lots of money and travelling. He protected me always and I looked out for him.

He was a cheeky fucker!!!! He ALWAYS had an answer ready and quite the whip when he was on one! TJ loved to have a drink and took to smoking like a natural. I do know that he didn't dabble in hard drugs. He had a good relationship with Mama but held very little respect for Toni. The last time Toni raised his hand to Mama at the dining table TJ stood up and guarded her. He loved the family and protected us all. He also warned off a few local guys from Teresa; letting them know in no uncertain terms that if they even so much as looked at her he would pulverise them. He had his own rules which meant that it was alright for him to sniff around their sisters but they were to leave his alone. He knew very many girls too, he was forever trying to set me up on dates with as many as he could, but I never took him up on them. He would grow up to be my closest friend and my loving brother. However, the future would hold some rough times for us. We had lots in common, he liked to dance and could move quite well, and he could sing rather well too. He liked football but not enough to support any particular team. He was often lazy with his priorities and boy could he talk the hind legs off a zebra.

TERESA

Teresa was Mama's second child and eight years older than me. She had traditional Greek features and speaks fluent English and Greek. She had natural curly brown hair which when lightened by the sun revealed a beautiful red hue. She was a very strikingly beautiful woman. You would never see her without a smile, not one of those fake smiles but a genuine inviting smile. She was a wonderful playmate and friend to me and she liked everything I did. We would play football and hang about the beach, running in and out of the limpet pools, crab fishing in the little pools. Mama has photographs of us with our fishing nets in our hands trying to catch the crabs there. They were happy days for me. She would protect me from others and always make sure Mama made my sandwiches small enough for me to eat. Sometimes she would allow me to paint her nails and fix her hair. We had such wonderful times together.

Teresa was an A1 student in housekeeping. From a very young age, girls were taught to cook and clean and look after their brothers, sisters, and anyone else who happened to pop by. So living with Mama and the clean freak she was, Teresa was not going to get away with not following Mama's example.

She was a clean girl too, kept herself to herself, didn't tease the boys or fool around. Teresa was a proud person and wanted a good career. She was not very close to Toni and as best she could, she kept her distance from him. As with everyone, she did have a lot of time for Riki, they both used to laugh and be serious at the same time. He so studious and she being quite smart for a girl always hung on to Riki's coat tails as if he was her idol, but she had less time for TJ. Amongst her peers, she was quite popular and had many friends. She was not a person to beat about the bush, she told things as she saw them and that is what endeared her to people. You would always be sure of getting the truth from Teresa. I think she would have gone on to be a good mum herself as she was almost a mini Mama, but as I said previously she wanted a career. We didn't know what career she had in mind yet but it would come out in the future, as she was a strong willed person and usually got what she wanted in the end in an almost professional manner. Following Mama, she developed a sense of leadership but gentle with it and was one of those people you instantly warmed to. She would tell you her life story warts and all and would become the best friend you could imagine always keeping quiet about other peoples business and never letting a word of privacy leave her lips. I will tell you what though; she couldn't half pack a punch. I would NOT like to get on the wrong side of her. I have been on the receiving end of one of her punches and believe me it is not pretty. Still she gave a lot of her time to others and cared very deeply, sometimes I think maybe too deeply. She taught me how to wear mascara and eyeliner and how to co-ordinate my colours better. She did not smoke or drink at all. Maybe seeing Toni being drunk a lot swayed her from that path.

So there you have it! My family, the people who have helped me along the way of my life to become the person I am today. They were the crazy people with who I grew up! I think you could have called us a clean and decent family; Mama had raised us with standards, manners and morals. We had the most beautiful and welcoming home, a place where anyone would want to be whether family or not. Living on the island was almost heaven. I don't think I could ever be any other place than here. We struggled as a family, the money was short but Mama always made sure we had what we wanted. I remember Mama having it hard when Toni was messing around, but as we grew older we all helped Mama pay the bills when we could afford to.

CHAPTER 3

SASKIA

The preceding is an introduction to my family and friends and how they helped shape me into the person I am today. It also gives you the area I grew up in and how I discovered dance, and also how my friends and family treated me once I "came out". The story I tell you shows you how things are not always what they seem and how my ideal life would turn from heaven to a living hell almost overnight.

Saskia was born of German and English parents and her father being in the army was based in Greece. Saskia's father was never at home much and her mother was quite a selfish woman. When I first saw Saskia it was in the local Greek mini market. She was with her mother and me with my Mama. She was all of about 13 or 14 years of age blonde hair, blue eyes and dress sense, jeans and t shirts, a little make up and her ears pierced. Our mothers were talking about what was going on at the local youth centre and that is where Saskia and I first got introduced

"Saskia, this is Christian. Say hello!"

"Hello!" she replied.

Mama then told me to introduce myself, which I did. I nodded a little nervous of my disability but she was cool. We saw each other after that first meeting almost every day as we both detested school. We would spend a lot of our time chilling on the beach and going for long walks or hanging out at Mama's house. We became inseparable at times and we could really communicate. Her house would often be empty so she would spend more and more time with me and my family at home. Mama thought we were like girlfriend and boy friend and lots of people classed us as Bonnie and Clyde. We grew quite thick with each other. I wasn't that keen on her mother in fact Saskia and I used to chat about her on a regular basis. She wasn't very good looking but Saskia was and she had no time for Saskia, maybe she felt a little jealous of Saskia's looks. Saskia was an only child and after a while she became part of the furniture in our house, she was a spoilt bitch at home but in our house she was much nicer. She thought her mother was thick and an unfortunate looking woman and had a bad attitude to life. She was glad she didn't have any brothers or sisters and held no respect for her father who she very rarely saw anyway. At school she was "miss popular". Every Greek girl wanted to be like her and most of the Greek boys wanted to sleep with her.

I wasn't interested in Saskia in the way a 15 year old boy would be about a teenage girl, and one day while we were talking I signed to Saskia

"Oh! By the way I am gay!" Her reply which is Saskia all over

"So fucking what!"

We had many laughs together and became big rebels. We felt comfortable together and always supported each other. We would go into the nearest town on a weekend and shop together. I paid for my purchases but Saskia began shop lifting things. I don't know why she did it, possibly to give her a thrill.

And that is the way our relationship was, closer than close but without the intimacy of a physical relationship. She was often times dressed as a boy and did boy things which quite evened out the girliness in me. She was not stupid at all to start with; she did have a brain once. She always did well at school in her projects and her exams – when she was there! She was obviously the girl who always stood out as she had blonde hair and that was a rarity in Corfu; everyone seemed to be dark hair and dark eyes. She was very popular at school, most of the older Greek lads wanted to go out with her but she always refused and besides they had already been warned off by TJ. She was looking for someone more exciting, she had plans for her life and she wasn't going to let anyone change her goals, so she always told me.

I had kissed with Saskia a couple of times. I was being harassed by a girl on a certain night, so I asked Saskia to kiss me. Let me tell you she didn't need asking twice she dived right in tongues and all! It did nothing for me, I was not interested in Saskia at all in a girlfriend sort of a way and anyway she preferred the older guys.

"Shame you are gay Christian!" She would say to me "You have a very fit body"

"Shame you are not!" I replied "You are not so bad yourself!"

That was the sort of relationship we had. We often laughed a joke here and a joke there but caring very deeply about each other. There was something about her.

When she grew a little older I hardly saw her. She would turn up here and there but nothing was shared really we seemed to have drifted apart. I didn't know why but I was sure going to find out. Her body was maturing and getting bigger; which attracted all the male population, and she was beginning to learn what an affect her appearance was having on them. How she could use her body and her sexuality to get what she wanted. Her clothes became tacky and tarty and she was always caked in heavy make up which was not very expertly applied. Even I could do a better job than she could. I stood back one day and thought to myself "Oh my God! What has happened to that cute thirteen year old I met at the mini market?" It didn't seem that long ago when Saskia came over to Mama's house one day and she was as white as a snow flake. She was trembling and pacing the floor.....

"FUCKING HELL!!!!!!" She yelled tears streaming down her face "I skipped my period! I'm late! For fuck's sake! What the hell am I going to do!!!!!!!?" She bleated out.

"Are you sure Saskia?" I asked reeling from shock.

"OF COURSE I AM FUCKING SURE!!!!!!" She screamed at me.

"Hey! Sask! It's not my fault is it!?" I said louder to make myself heard.

"OH GOD! NO! Sorry Christian, sorry. You are right" She said beginning to calm down a bit. She kissed me on the forehead and walked out. She never ceased to amaze me.

She had many problems and never confided in me which confused me a bit. I thought we were closer than close. I knew she put herself about a bit but I always thought she had the sense to be safe, as in contraceptive ways. Her pregnancy worried me as she smoked like a trooper and loved to down a vodka or two and even sometimes as much as she could stand at times. I knew she had been dabbling in harder drugs too but I didn't know if she was an addict or not. All these things she could not afford to do with a child on board, and as she disappeared for days at a time how could I help her or advise her? She was just that type of girl she gave you all or nothing at all.

CHAPTER 4

DISCOVERY

———————————

I had never cared to look at the girls on the beach at all, it didn't appeal to me. I didn't date any of my sister's girlfriends either. I knew I was gay at a lot younger age than 15. I had just decided to let every one know who I was at that age. Mama says she already knew and she didn't seem to care at all. Toni just gave me a dirty look every time he saw me but I fucking hated him as you know so I didn't care two hoots about his feelings. He never showed emotions anyhow he was not even a human being I think. He was rude to my friends though and that bothered me, he assumed all the boys who came over were all gay and dirty like me! It answered every one's questions about me and Saskia maybe having a future together now. Riki didn't care to really say anything on the matter. He said he didn't want to ever see me with a guy full on kissing but he was ok with me and understood it's what I had to do. Teresa was no different to how she had always been and said it was more like having a sister growing up than another brother and she liked that. TJ couldn't deal with the fact that I had decided to be openly gay, he had decided that I was disgusting and disowned me. After my revelation we had confrontations which always ended up in a fight, he was very cruel at times even spitting on me when he couldn't think of any particular derogatory words to use. As a response and given my frustration I could be just as cruel back. We would stare at each other with anger and cruel intentions. We deliberately ran into each other physically to try and start a fight, but Mama was always there to step in and cool things down. Mama gave both of us a stern talking to and we decided to stay away from each other. At times he would look straight through me as if I didn't exist. I cannot begin to tell you how much this hurt me, as a result our family began to separate and soon TJ would leave and I wouldn't see him for many years. The neighbours in the village all got to know and I got some strange, weird and funny looks and actions!!! The older people of the village just stared at me and gave me a dirty look – which I laughed at .Who were they kidding!? Greeks fucking invented the gay community!!! My friends were all cool about it. I got called "pushti" (the Greek word for gay) a few times but it wasn't in bad form. I could be myself though and not have to worry about girls. I was never going to have to hide what I was and I was proud too.

As I said I was 15 when I decided to come out. My first experience was very eye opening. Boy, that afternoon was something else! His name was Dimitris which in Greek means "One who loves the earth". He was 17 years old and went to my old school. We used to hang around together when a few of us were bunking off school for the day, and we would all go hang out at the beach. He was hot looking and we always eyed each other up in our swimwear, swam together and we could speak to each other too.

We spent a lot of time at my place too, just hanging out and playing music in the "Den". Oh the Den was my place – it was like a big outhouse that I had made into a place where I could go and listen to my music and practice dance with out being disturbed. It was some times a place I could go hide away to escape the bedlam going on all around. It had two large mirrors on the wall from ceiling to floor; all practicing dancers had at least one where they could practice. The walls were all painted in white and the wood flooring was red. It had three large, heavy bean bag cushions laid on the floor, blue, red and orange! It had a small table that was just covered in music tapes and articles I had cut out of the local dance newspapers. No one really came down to bother me here either.

Dimitris was a true Corfiot, born in the same village as me. His mother ran a bar in the high street and his father travelled a lot. He attended the same dance club I did. This one particular evening I had invited a few of the guys from the dance club to join me in my den to practice some dance and chill out. Dimitris was the last one left after about an hour of messing around and an hour of serious dance practice. We were lying on the bean bag cushions sipping coke and looking at each other.

He pulled out a built joint and said "Is it ok if I light up?"
"Yes" I nodded.

He smoked on it for a while and then passed it to me. I had never smoked dope before; I had only seen it and smelt it. With that he came over and sat beside me. I had smoked a few cigarettes before but this was amazing. I was so light headed and just kept on smiling and I didn't even know why! He lent over and kissed me on my mouth and how I liked it. We kissed and kissed and then we kissed some more. Before I knew it he had his hand down the front of my joggers doing – OH MY GOD! – Well use your imagination will you! We explored each others bodies for hours. I wouldn't say we were in love at all, just finding out what was nice and felt good. We didn't date either just hung out.

My clothes became more flamboyant when I "came out". I loved wearing pinks and whites, my t-shirts tight showing every ripple of my body. I then got as liking for piercings and got my ears done – yes both and my navel, my tongue and my left nipple. I loved showing off my new and open image. I was sexy and I knew it and flaunted myself about to catch the guys' eyes! Women did their fair of looking too, and they flirted with me quite a bit. It seemed that every woman who made a pass at me thought they were the one to "change" my lifestyle.

CHAPTER 5

DANCING

At about five years old I had been playing in the house one day. I hadn't paid any attention before but I began to get a strange feeling in my feet on the wooden floors in the lounge. It was what can only be described as a tingling under my feet. I placed my hands on the floor where the feeling was coming from. It felt like ripples moving across the palms of my hands. It felt very strange and as I moved my hands I was directed to a table upon which sat a machine which Mama explained was called a "music machine". I had obviously seen the machine before but on this particular day I was very curious about how my feet and hands felt and wanted to know more. The closer my hands got to the machine the more intense the feelings became. As I got to the machine there was a feeling in my hands that was more of a "bang bang" against them. I placed one hand on the machine and every hair in my body stood on end as if I was having an electric shock. The bangs on my hand began to happen in a pattern and Mama told me it was called rhythm and that if I could hear I would be listening to music. The more I held my hands there the more I enjoyed it. Mama was standing in the doorway of the kitchen wiping her hands on her apron watching me. She could see music was beginning to have a wonderful effect on me. This one day she stepped forward to turn a knob on the music machine. As she did so the feelings became stronger and stronger. I was starting to feel the beat and began to bend my knees and clap my hands. All of a sudden I began to move to the music. Mama was so pleased with me and ran around the room clapping her hands and jumping in the air. The expression on her face was beautiful, she looked so happy, I think it was at that moment that my life was about to change for the better. What I had discovered was "Dance". I felt so emotional at how happy I had made Mama.

Even though I couldn't hear the music I had the beat and rhythm in my head and from that time I would always be seen dancing around the house. I began to watch dancing on the TV as Mama would turn the sound up so I could feel the vibrations in the floor. I would sit for hours and watch these people putting their bodies into all sorts of shapes and in time with the music. I knew I could do what these dancers were doing and from that moment my life was music and dance. Yes, the house used to be very loud, especially in my room but it didn't bother Mama she was just happy that I had found something that I loved and had a natural ability to do.

Once I had learnt how to move to the music I would become a constant source of "entertainment" within the neighbourhood; especially when Mama had one of her "gatherings" at home.

As my talent improved Mama began entering me into local competitions which occurred every so often in the village. She would help me hone my dance skills and I would practice every day to make up a routine. My first competition happened when I was six years old. The atmosphere was electric. There were a few competitors but they were all girls. All dressed in fancy clothes and a great deal of make up on their faces. They seemed to have everything I didn't. Our family finances were not that good so I asked for dance clothes for my birthday and was happy to receive my first pair of proper dance shoes. This was the best present I had ever had. Now I was able to move properly to the music.

It was a summer's afternoon on a Saturday and we all met at the community centre for the competition. The girls were all giggling and flouncing about in their costumes. I had on black shorts and a black T-Shirt with white ankle socks and my prized possession, my beautiful dancing shoes. My main rival was Sophia Kanakaredes, she was pretty, I will give her that, but she was so far up herself that she looked at me as if I was the dirt she had picked up off her shoe. I caught her eye and she had such a smug look on her face, I smiled at her and she just gave me such a snotty look that my face changed and if I could I would have jumped straight on her to wipe the look off her face. Who was she to look at me like that! I was the last to dance, I started to get a bit nervous as all the competitors before me were pretty good, and even though I hate to admit it even Sophia was quite good. It came to my turn and I stood on the stage shaking. The music started and I felt the stage vibrate, this was my cue, I tapped my foot a couple of times to get the rhythm and then I was off! I forgot everyone was there and just danced how I did in my room in private. I finished my number and opened my eyes and there in front of me the whole of the hall was standing and clapping. Wow! This was more than I expected. The judges sat at a table in front of the stage and there seemed to be a bit of a kafuffle, they were all leaning in to each other and smiling, nodding their heads and papers were flying. They signalled the director and all the competitors were brought back on stage. We were all lined up and the results were read out. "In third place…..Antonia Paulou." She was brought forward and given her trophy and a bunch of flowers. "In second place………Sophia Kanakaredes" She too was brought forward and given her trophy and flowers. The look on her face was as if someone had just smacked her. She obviously thought that she was the best, but she didn't take her loss too easily. "And in first place …………………………..Christian Miyarou!" The place erupted in applause. I was completely shocked and the look that Sophia gave me was so sick I would have been buried six feet under. She hated me from that minute and we were always rivals in these competitions. We never spoke to each other; it was just the looks that passed between us which told each other how we felt.

That trophy was the first of many to adorn a shelf in my room. The cash prize of 50 Drachma I gave to Mama. Every contest that came up I would be there with the family in tow. I felt sometimes as if I was being a bit unfair on the other contestants as I always ended up walking away with the cash prize. This prize was not for me but for Mama the light of my life, she usually ended up buying her cigarettes with it as it was never enough to take her away on a holiday which she richly deserved. I didn't like her smoking as I worried about her health. She had a terrible hacking cough most of the time. But Mama did what Mama did. She loved us all but I always felt more special because she seemed to be always there for me and gave me love like no other could. Living in our home was not easy for Mama, she had to work and care for us all and without the help of Toni, who was a bit selfish and kept all his money for himself. Poor Mama she did try very hard. Mama was beaming with pride and it was at that moment I felt I had found my destiny. Each competition that came up over the next few years was won by me and Sophia was always second. It was a fierce competition between us. The mothers began to show their feelings and one of them said to Mama at the end of the competition "He should go to dance classes. He is very talented. That way it would give some of the others a chance. This is too easy for Christian, he has a rare talent and will go a along way with the right direction.

That evening when we returned home and Mama sat me down in the lounge. She asked me if I would like to learn many more types of dance. I was about ten years old at this time. I felt that the competitions were too easy but I didn't want to give up. Mama said she felt it was time for me to try something a bit harder. She explained there was a lady in the neighbourhood who taught others how to dance.

The very next Saturday Mama and I made our way to meet my new dance teacher. Her name was Ms Buddana. She was a small elderly lady but had the patience of a saint. She dressed in a typically Greek way, in black, with her grey hair tied behind her head in a knot and carried a stick which she used to tap on the floor in time with the music, she was a force to be reckoned with but got the best out of her pupils and earned a great deal of respect in the neighbourhood.

We walked into the hall where she taught. I was a little nervous but excited and held Mama's hand securely. The butterflies in my stomach were flying madly. I took my steps one by one into the hall and looked up and around. The hall had mirrors along one wall and the music was piped through a sound system which echoed and vibrated so that I could feel it. As I walked around the hall I could see myself in the mirrors. Ms Buddana disappeared through a door and the next thing I was tapping my feet to the music. The ripples I felt urged me to close my eyes and all of a sudden Mama let go of my hand. I felt someone touch my elbow, I opened my eyes and saw Mrs Buddana. She was so gentle and a smile on her face assured me that all was well. We had eye contact and she mouthed to me to dance.

"Let yourself feel the music and show me what you can do" she said. I felt her hit the floor with her stick in time with the music. I closed my eyes again and was transported to another world where it was just me and the sun.

During my dancing sessions I would wear loose fitting clothing – jogging bottoms and socks over the top of the ankles to keep everything in place, and shorts. This had to be the way it was until I either earned some money or Mama could afford to buy me the proper clothing. I danced barefoot so that I could feel the vibrations better, each note sending shocks up my legs that sent me into a whirlwind of dance. There were not many stipulations about clothing as every one mainly, was in the same boat as finances were concerned. Barefoot dancing made me feel free as a bird and as I danced I felt as if I was flying.

I learnt many types of dance with Mrs Buddana and we became quite close. She was something of a perfectionist and pushed me very sternly to work hard. It wasn't long before I became her star pupil and she always used me as an example to the others when they couldn't get the steps right. I was a sucker for attention so I didn't mind at all. Whenever there was a new step to learn she would teach me first. Dancing came naturally for me and I would simply watch her and then copy her moves, most of the time I got it right first time. She taught me to dance for three years up until the time of her death. She died one night in her sleep from natural causes. I was very sorry to see her go she had so much patience for me and I always felt very safe when I was around her. She taught me the amazement of tap and jazz with mellow tunes and superb tempos. She also taught me how to dress up properly and to make up when it was appropriate, how to stand correctly and how to move well. She always insisted on us warming up before class started and I still continue to do this before I do any dancing. It is very important for the body to be warmed up or you could have a serious accident and I would have to stop dancing, so I wasn't going to allow that to happen. The lessons that Mrs Buddana taught me have stood me in good stead for my career, and what I gained from her I passed on to my pupils after I started my own dance school. Mrs Buddana was a wonderful woman and taught me many things besides dance. She taught me gymnastics to improve my balance.

My disability was no barrier to what I wanted to do, I fought hard to get to the top of my profession and I WAS going to succeed. I was good at dancing and I knew it. My communication to the world came through my love of dance. This was the way I was going to give Mama back everything she gave to me. She was my life and I was to be ever grateful for her being my mother. What a wonderful woman.

I went for my first dancing job when I was 17. At the time I was still attending the dance club with my friends. A bar in the next village was advertising for a dancer, it sounded out of the way so I thought that maybe I could give it a go! Mama would not think anything out of the ordinary as I told her I would be working in the town. A bar job was all she needed to know.

The bar looked pretty clean and unlike some of the rough bars around. It was quite a big place with the traditional flower baskets hanging outside the entrance and the name of the bar was "Adonis". It had plenty of umbrella'd tables with enough seating arranged to allow all who ventured there to be comfortable. Lights were everywhere lighting up the outside patios where many, many people mingled to enjoy their nights out. The inside, however, was quite different. I had never been to this place before and was quite shocked at how many people and who were the same as me. There were groups of guys with guys, girls with girls and many mixed groups of both sexes. Nothing was held back in there it seemed like a "free for all" place. One I was happy to become a part of. There were guys kissing guys, girls kissing girls. There was a podium in the centre which was attached to the stage and led to the back where the dressing rooms were.

As I entered the bar with much trepidation, I saw a big fat Greek man at the bar. He looked disgusting, which did not go together with the standard of the place. He had longish dirty coloured greasy, slicked back hair, an untended moustache and looked like he hadn't had a shave in a month of Sunday's. He looked, what I would call "smelly", and wore a pale blue striped shirt undone a few buttons and let his hairy chest show, the buttons were straining to expose the flab beneath the shirt. I can tell you it didn't appeal to me at all; he really did look like he didn't belong in a fine establishment as this one. He lent over the bar as was talking to the barman and a couple of his friends who surprisingly were well kept and smart looking.

I walked over to the bar after I had asked one of the waitresses where the bar owner was. Unfortunately she had pointed to the man I noticed when I walked in. I introduced myself and he shook me by the hand and said

"Hello" in a gruff voice and looking at me in what can only be described as a very weird way.

"I am Spyros and what can I do for you young man?"

I didn't like the way he was looking at me and felt very uncomfortable. As he was looking at me I cast my eyes over the interior of the bar and noticed penis ornaments everywhere, lined up all along the bar behind the bar staff. Pictures of nakedness hung haphazardly on the walls. The clientele were wearing the wildest clothes and in some cases as little clothing as it seemed they could possibly get away with, without losing a certain amount of modesty. He explained to me that yes there was a position available and that I had the body for what he had in mind. He took me to the back of the stage in his office where he asked me to do a small audition for him. I was nervous but I needed the job and as it was dancing I felt I had nothing to lose and possibly everything to gain. As I danced I saw him watching me and he was getting quite excited, this put me in a bit of a panic as I felt as if he was going to make a pass at me.

"You look very nice and you move really well. You really do have rhythm in you I am sure we can do business." He said to me as the music stopped.

"Thank you!" I replied

"When would you want to start?" He asked. I paused for a moment and then he asked "How about this Friday night? I have some costumes in the back for you to wear and the guys and girls will help you with whatever you need."

I accepted his offer and felt pretty good although a little concerned still about the way he was looking at me. Did he have plans? Was he a weirdo? And worst of all "did he FANCY me!!!!!?" God I hoped not he was not very nice and certainly wasn't my type of man. I left Adonis and went home thinking about the place all the time. It seemed very interesting and easy money was to be had, and this I needed for Mama.

Friday came and I went to work, I told Mama that I had a job in town just to keep her happy. She would not be amused about where I was going to work, so for the time being I kept it a secret from her. I hated keeping secrets from Mama, as when she found out something I had done and I had kept it secret she usually went ballistic in her Greek way, arms flailing, and chest beating. I could just imagine it now "OH!!! Christian!!! Why you do this to your Mama huh! Why you make you lookin' cheap?" I really couldn't handle that at the moment. I arrived at Adonis and went to the dressing room at the back. You notice I say dressing room and not dressing rooms, the reason being that it was a communal dressing room and everyone's boas and sparkles were hanging all over the place. The room was dimly lit but each dressing table around the room had its own large mirror with the lights all around the outside. This was to enable us all to do our make up, and I watched intently for a while as the guys were putting on their full face of make up. I made my way through all the finery and found my costume. Well if you can call it a costume! There was barely anything to it just a black g-string style pair of shorts. I took one look and thought to myself "HELP!!!!" How the hell was I going to wear this? I sat for a while and pondered over what I was letting myself in for. Still all the time in the back of my mind was Mama and how much I needed to help her.

After a short while I took hold of the "shorts" and worked out what way they were to go on. There was no privacy really, unless you went into the toilets, so I stripped off. I have to say one or two pairs of eyes made their way to looking at me. Strangely enough though, they didn't make me feel like the boss Spyro did. I guess we were all in the same boat. I was lent a bottle of oil by one of the guys and he showed me how to rub it in to my body to get the full effect. I tried to get ready as quickly as I could to save any embarrassment but without any warning my music played. The track was from an album by George Michael, one of my favourite artists. The girls started to panic and almost literally pushed me out the curtains on to the stage. I took a look at what lay before me and panicked for a split second, then I got the beat in my feet and I started to move. As I began to writhe around the pole, I saw how my movements were affecting some people. I smiled a knowing smile and took hold of the pole. Hmmm! I was beginning to enjoy this. Being up on the stage looking down I felt as if I had power somehow. A power that I knew would one day stand me in good stead and hopefully further my dance career. The heat made the oil on my body glisten as it mixed with the sweat I had from the lights all focusing on me. I certainly felt powerful and just leant into the music and lost myself. As I came closer to the punters around the stage I had people putting notes in my shorts. WOW! I thought this IS easy money! They could look but they were not permitted to touch unless to put notes in my shorts that is. Whilst dancing on the podium, men would lean forward and try and touch me while I danced and offered me money to go "out back for some extras" along with drugs. I didn't tell Mama how horrible the people really were at the club as she would have worried for me and this was my time to fend for myself and try and deal with people. She would never have agreed to let me keep dancing if she had known what I was doing and how I was being treated but I had to keep on dancing it was fast becoming my life and I had to learn to take the rough with the smooth if I was ever to succeed.

Later on after I had finished my set I would watch from behind the curtains and everyone was drunk and high on drugs. Some were regulars, every night they would appear with the same intentions as the night before. It always surprised me, did they never get bored? I guess that would be a "NO!" I didn't want to get into what these guys were into after taking the drugs they bought there. Some were just passers by but everyone who came in single went out partnered. It had a magical feel about it. Everyone danced and went crazy, and made as much noise as they could. People hugged and kissed, heavy snogging is what we called it. This behaviour continued every night even with people jumping up on to the tables and dancing themselves silly. The same men would try to catch me at least every other day; many of them were persistent and would not give up. They took pictures of everyone even the dancers; however, I did not like my picture being taken as I knew these men would then go home and have a filthy wank over them. I was getting quite well known in the dancing clubs in and around my area.

The customers at the bar were quite wealthy and they felt they could own me for their money. I would dance and strip but I drew the line at prostituting myself. It may be a fine line between stripping and prostituting but for me there was a big difference. I began to resent the men who felt they could literally buy me. They had more money than they knew what to do with. They would wear expensive designer clothes and manage to come across looking like someone better in a street person's rags. Many of them would live in these bars, staying drunk then sleeping it off and coming back to the bar with only a splash of cheap cologne to cover the stale smell of cigars and alcohol from the many nights before. I wondered if they bathed once a month, once a year or indeed ever. Some people thought I should be the one to feel dirty but actually I was there to gain experience dancing and this was simply a means to an end, a way for me to gain experience and to earn money to further my career. These rich men were the ones who seemed to me dirty and didn't have a life. I don't mean to sound cruel but they would think of me as property to be bought and sold. I laughed inside sometimes, how they could think that I was the dirty one baffled me.

Many times men would bring their partners so they could watch the dancing and get their wives and girlfriends all excited, get themselves worked up and then go home and have nights of passion on my performance. It is hard to describe how I felt about this but in some way I was flattered, but it made me feel sad also. The main thing for me was that I got to dance and go home at night with a satisfaction that I had thrilled the people who attended the club. I learnt a lot about people too, the way they looked at me when I danced and stripped for them enlightened me into their characters. Through watching them watching me perform I learnt how to read people and I knew this would stand me in good stead for the future and how I would learn to trust or not trust people with whom I came into contact in my everyday life. It really was a learning curve for me.

Many older men would come to the club looking to pick up younger men. They would settle for either a "hand job" in their cars or oral sex in some dark alley. Many of the guys who danced there were into this kind of thing but I wasn't. I just felt powerful watching them and knowing what I did to them gave me a bit of a thrill.

As I looked out on the crowd I felt as if I was in charge. Never before had I ever had such a feeling. I looked at the faces and thought how sad they were, not in an unhappy way but in a way that they were all lusting after me and getting turned on by what they saw me do. What sort of life did they have paying to watch guys and girls in all sorts of scant costumes performing in front of them for them to get their rocks off! The clothes they wore were of a fine quality and attending the bar and watching the performances didn't come cheap either. Drugs were being handed round like sweets, but I always stayed away from that. I didn't want to become a freak and become dependent on some stimuli to be the person I truly was. I was quite gregarious and with my talent and seeing how the people liked what I did and wanted more, was more than enough of a drug for me. After that first night I earnt some good money and it was easy. I was in control on the podium so I only took off what I wanted but they still stood there shouting for more. I thought, why give them everything, if I did that at the beginning of my act there would be nothing left for later. I worked in Adonis three nights a week.

As I left in the early hours I counted the money I had made and knew that Mama would be pleased I had brought home something for the "pot". But had she known what I had done to earn it she would have had a hissy fit!

After a few weeks Mama started to question where the money was coming from along with bunches of flowers that were sent to her. The money became more and more as I became increasingly more popular in the Adonis.

The men in the bar – the regular ones – would ask me to go outside and earn "extras" with them but I continually said no! I wasn't into giving a quick blow job in a car or up some alleyway. I tried to steer clear of them; sometimes they would offer me work at private parties. I had one client who invited me to his house on a regular basis to dance for his guests wearing next to nothing. The rich men and women loved to touch me up and place money in my clothing, whatever I had on at the time, but this was always a good earner.

I stayed at the Adonis for about a year and along with the private parties I really enjoyed it and earnt a fair whack. However, doing this work in secret had its drawbacks. I would wander around the village and look at people, some I took as looking at me strangely but I think I was possibly a bit paranoid thinking "OH MY GOD! I HOPE THEY DON'T RECOGNISE ME!!!!! But counting up the pros and cons of the lifestyle I wasn't that bothered, I was good at what I did and I was earning really good money.

The inevitable day arrived when Mama found out what I was doing. She pitched a right fit when she found out I was taking my clothes off! She blessed herself a hundred times screaming at me.

"Why Christian? Why!!!!! Why would you do it! You are beautiful young man. You have much to offer. Why you sink so low to take your clothes off. People no respect you now. You such a good boy! I never to walk in village no more with head held high!"

She paced the floor back and forth, back and forth, babbling in Greek a hundred miles an hour, or what seemed like it. Every time I opened my mouth to talk she started again. Still I should have learnt by now when Mama was on one to leave her to it until she calmed down. After a while she calmed down and said there was no harm in what I was doing, simply dancing; which I enjoyed and it was easy money. All that fuss for nothing!

My plans for having my own business were starting to take shape. With the money I earnt I would put some aside to enable me to one day open up my own dance studio. I wanted to help other children in the same position as me to try something that would make their lives a bit better. I wanted to help them be confident human beings whether able-bodied or disabled, and have, hopefully, a career themselves one day.

CHAPTER 6

JAY

———————

Jay was your average forty year old American taking his yearly vacation on the Emerald Isle of Corfu. He was about six feet tall with short brown hair and he wore glasses. He wasn't the best looking guy I had ever met but he held a kindness to his face. A smile warm and inviting with eyes deep and genuine, and which he fixed on me. He wore blue trousers with a flowing light baby blue shirt and leather sandals. He carried a rucksack on his arm full of things like maps and a camera with spare films. He had never ventured out of America before and came to Greece alone to explore the sights and history of my home. He had been married to a woman for many, many years but the marriage did not have children. He worked in the local hospital to where he lived in the States as a nurse. This showed me how compassionate a man he was, caring and gentle.

I was helping out in the local family run restaurant - it was not my normal type of job as you know but they were under staffed this certain night so I was asked by Mama to help out and wait and clean the tables – normally by the end of the night I would be dancing on them!! It was a cool way to earn some money and also show off my skills in dance. I liked to show off that way. When the season started the tourists came in droves to be fed the national dishes of Greece.

Well to carry on with Jay!! I do get carried away sometimes about myself I know!! It was a beautiful August night and he was having a meal at the most famous "Faros" restaurant. It was a huge place where you could grab a meal out side under the pagoda overlooking the Ionian Sea, or, you could stay inside and prop up a bar or just flaunt yourself all over the dance floor which I often did! He was waiting for service and he got me. He seemed to pick up straight away that I had a hearing disability but this did not fault him at all – He moved his lips in a way I could read them and ordering his meal was easy. We smiled at each other often during the course of the evening. By the end of the night I found myself sitting at his table having conversations with him – well some things were being written down and small hand signs were happening naturally but we conversed nonetheless. It was quite amazing – like we had known each other all our lives really. He explained to me that he was interested in seeing lots of nearby places and I offered to take him around. He was delighted with this offer and jumped on a YES straight away. We decided to meet the very next day at the life guards post on the beach which was not too far from Faros.

He told me his name was Jeremy but I could not pronounce that very well so I called him Jay. He was delighted. We both arrived on time. The morning was a beautiful one – the sun was out a just a little cloud overhead, like wisps of grey hair on a little old lady.

The sea was calm and the beach was beginning to get filled with people gathering their sun loungers and "saving" their spots before the beach got full. The beach was amazing to me so I thought it would be a good start to Jay's journey. We sat on the sand watching the sea side by side. He was wearing a flowing white cotton shirt with white ¾ length cottons on with white flip flops. He looked fresh and clean and he smelled nice too. I wore a white vest t shirt with blue denims and white pumps. I had my sunglasses on too – of course I didn't venture far with out those on. Every time I said his name "Jay" he would look at me and smile overwhelmed by my nickname for him, his smile so appreciative. We had a great deal of eye contact as being deaf I had to read peoples faces and lips to work out what they were saying. But the eye contact grew more often stares which made me sometimes blush and him chuckle. God I liked him - really did like his company and he made me feel warm and safe inside and I felt he was crazy about me. We went for a walk along the beach and came to the Canal d'amour. Local folklore says a person looking for their true love must swim around the rock naked and would then find them. The water was so deep around the base of the rocks that it splashed up the side of them and became quite dangerous. Many swimmers would be thrown against the rocks and often were killed. If you look up the steep side you will notice various plaques with dedications on them of people who had died trying to swim as the legend told. Often there would be people who would jump off the rocks in an act of suicide usually over forlorn love. The place was beautiful and reminded me of a scene from "Jason and the

Argonauts where Poseidon is holding the rocks open for the Argo to travel through. It was a mystical place and one we felt comfortable in. We took many pictures and during our lunch we would sit on the beach and watch people swimming and having an enjoyable time.

After our time together I introduced him to some of my friends who I played pool with and chilled with. I introduced him to Saskia who liked him too, which was surprising as she normally hated any strange man near me. Whilst having one of our many conversations in getting to know each other we talked about our previous relationships. He told me that he and his wife had a strange type of relationship. They had never had any children and Jay always felt that it was this that was lacking in their marriage. Nothing was holding them together but the piece of paper signed in courthouse he went his way and she went hers. She wasn't into travelling or eating foreign dishes and trying new things so he was glad she did not come on this venture with him and so was I.

Jay tried to teach me to speak. I was astounded really because nobody had tried to teach me how to speak like a normal person; they just assumed that I wouldn't be able to do it. Well, Jay sat with me patiently and taught me how to bring sounds up from my diaphragm rather than just blowing air across my teeth and lips. I don't think he really knew how much he had inspired me. When he returned home I would phone him and in my limited speech would call his name "Jay Jay Jay" Mama would take the phone off me as I couldn't hear what he was saying and she would tell me what he had said. He was so excited that I had made the effort to talk to him. From that time I began to try and speak, it didn't quite sound right to start with but I knew with this as I knew with everything that

I would eventually get the hang of it and before long I would be able to communicate in a way I had never done so before. Wow! I had found my voice and I was so excited. The fortnight I spent with Jay made me feel the happiest man alive.

I met him for three days consecutively and on the fourth day I took him home to meet Mama and the family! OMG! You should have seen Mama! She cleaned the house from top to bottom every nook and cranny she could find was cleaned. She cooked a wonderful traditional Greek dinner. There was Spetzofia – a spicy sausage with peppers, also a roasted pork shoulder stuffed with cheese, you have to taste that it is positively orgasmic!

An ornate crisp, white tablecloth lay atop the table scattered with many dishes; Greek salad ladled with feta and tzatziki along with pitta breads. The meal was a meal to be proud of and done in the style only Mama lays on. For desert we had the best dish ever! Kormos, it was the best you would ever taste anywhere in the world. It is rather like a rum chocolate cake, which once you had one piece you wanted more. Mama was in her glory! She would be able to go a gossiping in the mini market with the older Greek moose's chatting about how she had cooked for an American – she would be the talk of the town! She really made a big fuss of Jay and he fell in love with her humour and wit and in turn all the family took to Jay. Mama was dumbfounded that I was actually learning to speak and that Jay had been teaching me. I was so proud to call her my Mama and put my arm across her shoulder bringing her to me and kissing her on the forehead. She had done me proud and made Jay feel comfortable in our home.

At the end of that night I walked Jay back to his holiday apartment, which was not too far from the high street. He invited me in for a night cap and told me that I didn't have to go in if I didn't want to, but I did – Oh God! I so did – SO I DID!

We sat in the small back yard he had and we sipped lemonade. I rolled up a joint – which he laughed at. He smoked cigarettes but would not touch the dope but he was cool I did it. We kicked back together side by side and gazed at the stars. That's the moment I faced him and looked at him right into his eyes and he looked kind of sad. He explained that he would be going back to USA to sort out his affairs with his wife and he wanted to divorce her. He knew he was gay and always had been and had lived a lie for many a long year – He told me my brevity had made him see sense and he wanted to come out. I just looked at him and I smiled. He made me smile a lot. I really liked him for that. I asked him if I could stay the night there with him I was so comfortable in his company I didn't want it to ever end but I knew it would when it was time to go home for him and that was coming soon. He had never been physical with a male before. I told him I wanted to stay the night and he was so nice: reassuring me all the time – was I ok? Did I want a drink? Did I want go out side for a smoke? - And so on.

I took him by the hand and said "Come on Jay" and walked towards the bathroom. He took my other hand and followed. I started to take off my clothes in front of him and he stared at me looking over my body. I did not have trouble taking off my clothes in front of people at all, I was proud of what my body looked like I had worked hard to get it in good shape. I could not hide the fact I was excited and this appealed to him and it became so natural to him then. We entered the shower together laughing at first because the water hadn't heated up yet! We kissed and we held on to each other tight.

The water was running over us both and we just held on to the moment.............it was beautiful. We then fumbled our way together kissing and walking backwards bumping into walls trying to find the bedroom! God we laughed so much and that made it so special. Eventfully we found our way and we hit the bed. Oh my God we were about to give our bodies and our love to each other and we so wanted to. We spent hours kissing and touching each other and just exploring. We smiled constantly eye to eye and the lights were on. Looking at my eyes his gaze was deep. I loved the way we communicated with our eyes. He was such a gentle gentleman. He was so sincere and innocent. His touch made me shiver. He held my face and said, "Christian, I am giving myself to you, take me and make me your man!" This was serious stuff. I penetrated him with such care; I did not want to hurt him or myself. Our love making was slow and meaningful. I had now planted my seed deep into him, he would always bare love for me, and I was his first. Our love making lasted hours that night and we both crashed contented lying together like spoons closely fitted very snug. Man this felt so good – safe.

We woke together and cuddled up in his duvet – or comforter as he called it! It felt nice to wake up to his warm body with a nice smile and a "good morning hunny" I loved his humour, he was always trying to make me laugh by doing silly things. I had to do something special for him before he went back to America.

Jay informed me that he was going to have to go back to his home at the end of the week.

"I don't want to go now Christian you do know that don't you" he said looking in my eyes in his soft tone. I searched for answers in his eyes but deep down I knew he had to go. Time had passed so fast. There was still so much I wanted to show Jay and take him to other villages... Time didn't wait around. It was as if the last week of his vacation had just flown by.

I had arranged for all the family to be in Faros and all my friends too – I was going to put on a night of gratitude and thanks for Jay. He meant so much to me. This parting was going to be painful for both of us. I had all the traditional foods cooked for him. He had found a love for clefticoe since being in Greece so I made sure the best was prepared for him. The tables were full of fresh fruits, salads and Greek cakes. There were champagne glasses filled with bubbles sitting on trays just waiting to be picked up and drunk. Balloons everywhere with "Jay" printed on them. I knew that name had become special for him. The atmosphere was alive in there and it certainly was packed out. Every one seemed to have a liking for Jay. He was a very decent genuine man, one whom I would miss. I had practiced a dance to a very slow tempo (Imagine). I had been working on it for some time and I was going to dedicate this to Jay. He knew I could relate through my dance and music and when I had done he would see and feel my affection for him.

I waited for the music to start and the lights were dim. As it started I began to move my body – stretching and pirouetting, walking elegantly around the hall as the lights grew brighter. I looked at Jay with a loving warm smile; he smiled back all the way through it. The crowds were all smiling and cheering for every move I made, I would drop down into doing the splits and then seductively roll on the floor. I moved every part of my body to the music with all the emotion I could possibly share. Every body knew I was dancing for Jay.

The song "Imagine" became very special between Jay and I, he knew I was making a statement. He looked so right sitting with Mama and the family, he belonged. His smile was heart moving. He had found himself being here, and opened up to his true feelings. He said he had never been so free and happy. We danced together for the rest of the evening and mingled with the friends and family. We ate like lords and laughed so much. We decided to say goodnight to everyone around midnight and went for a walk to spend some time alone. Holding hands and just smiling we walked together on the sand. We did not have to talk we were so content. I laid my jacket on the sand and we sat together cuddling.

"I do have to leave tomorrow Christian, I really don't want to but I don't have a choice" he said looking into my eyes.

"I know Jay, I know" I replied.

We spent a little time just holding each other listening to the soft wind on the sea and then we made our way back to his apartment. As he opened the door the first thing I saw was two cases both packed, tagged and ready to go.

"Jay" I said

Yes hunny "he replied trying to overlook the cases.

"Hurry back "I added. He held me tight and I just clung on to him. We kissed frantically as if it was going to be our last kiss.

"No regrets Christian and no tears, every thing will be ok" he reassured me. We made love to each other for hour's infact to the early hours of the morning.

At about 10.30am we took a slow stroll along the shore line, funnily enough where our journey almost first started by the life saving posts. We cuddled without a care who was watching.

For two people only having just less than 2 weeks together we were happy and it felt quite amazing. We had clicked from the first moment we met and we had bonded almost immediately. I drove him to Sportera airport, checked in his cases and waited for his boarding time to show on the screen.

"Christian - thank you for the best time of my life" he continued

"I know what I have to do in life now and that's thanks to you, I am going to miss you Christian" and then the flight appeared on the screen, now boarding. This was it, he was going. I walked him as far as I could go and then we stopped and looked at each other. We hugged, we kissed and we knew people were staring but we didn't give a shit. I kissed him fully on his mouth and hoped it would last forever.

"I have to go now Christian, take care of yourself and thank you again for everything" he said

"No! – thank you Jay you inspire me to no ends" Then he walked through passport control. That was that. I could not see him any more.

I took a slow walk back to my car. I sat in that car for about 35 minutes and his plane took off and up in the air. I watched it till it disappeared.

I cried. My chest hurt deep inside and I had a lump in my throat. I think I may have fell in love with Jay. I wish I had told him.

Bye Jay ......

CHAPTER 7

SASKIA A MUM

The day soon came when I would see the onset of birth...

"AAAARRRRRRGGGGGGGGHHHHHHHH-HHH!!!!!!" I sensed something from the lounge. Being in the kitchen I dropped what I was doing and plates cascaded everywhere. I ran as fast as I could to the lounge and there sat Saskia on the sofa doubled up in pain, red faced and clammy screaming at me, a sound I was to continue hearing for the next few hours.

"IT FUCKING HURTS CHRISTIAN!!!!!" She screamed and in my opinion it sounded as if she was straining. The baby was coming that was sure! I grabbed her pre-packed hospital bag and threw it in the car. I went back to help Saskia as she took a few steps before the pains came back. They were getting stronger and stronger I could see by the look on her face. This was not the Saskia I knew, her face all screwed up and red going into purple. I had seen births on the television and had watched animals giving birth but now my heart was thumping as the blood ran coursing through my veins in panic stimulated by the adrenaline rush. Those things I saw on the television did not in any way compare to reality. I was basically shitting a brick! I helped Saskia into the car enduring unending bouts of verbal abuse from her. She called me all the pricks under the sun. For her safety and mine I had to get her to the hospital as soon as I could. Saskia was settled in the front passenger seat, which I was later to regret doing! Every time she grunted and moaned I cringed and held my breath waiting for the next onslaught of vile words coming from her mouth. She was holding on to the seat as if she was on a white knuckle ride at the fun fair. I mistakenly looked over to her as I heard another deep rooted groan come from her chest. I really felt as if I had the devil in my car! The look she gave was that of a woman possessed. Her eyes black and deep set getting blacker with each breath she took. She grabbed my arm as it rested on the gear shift. OMG!!!!!! What pain I endured! Her nails digging into my hand and drawing blood, the car swerving as she tried to grab my hand each time I threw her off. I tried with all my might to keep the car going, then the pain had started to ease and she released her grip. I shook the pain out of my hand put my foot to floor and drove like a mad man to get her to the hospital before all three of us were killed in an accident! After what seemed like a life time we arrived at the A & E entrance to the hospital. I ran like a headless chicken and grabbed the first person I could find in uniform. I found a young nurse and dragged her almost to the car in which Saskia what screaming at the top of her lungs. The nurse opened the door took one look and ran inside the emergency room. She located a doctor and a baby delivering kit. Obviously all the pains she was enduring was progressing the labour quite quickly. A wheelchair was brought out by a porter and hurrying alongside was the nurse I had grabbed a few moments before. The three of us helped Saskia into the chair so she could be taken to the delivery room I had paid for to enable her to have a quiet and peaceful delivery. She wouldn't let go of me, the porter pushed the chair and the young nurse scurried along beside her feet shuffling ten to the dozen and he uniform making a noise as her hips moved from side to side.

They had been moved into a beautiful room, well I was paying for it and I wanted nothing but the best for Saskia. The room was delicately painted and furnished, beautiful pale pink curtains with a dado rail going round the middle of the room, flowers adorning the side cabinet. A place of solitude for mum and baby to spend their first few hours together, safe and alone to get to know each other and form a bond that hopefully would never be broken. That was the future but for the time being Saskia was about to deliver her little bundle.

You could cut the atmosphere in the room with a knife. Saskia lay on the bed, face red as a ruby, and wet with perspiration as each contraction got harder and harder and more and more painful. It was a long eight hours and in that time Saskia had done very well in coping with the pain; mind you I don't think my hands would agree with that one, they were now dotted with tiny scabs where Saskia had dug her nails into them, she had only been administered one shot of pethidine and a full cylinder of gas and air. It seemed as if it was never ending. On and on the moans and screams went, I was getting worried as to how much more she could cope with, I bathed her brow and shoulders and neck in a nice cold flannel, and she was sweating hard and seemed to appreciate that. She pulled my hair, she ripped my shirt and she bit my finger. Then came the doctor to check and he uttered those words every woman is petrified to hear.

"You are fully dilated and now you can start to push" The doctor said to Saskia looking at his eyes so she had something to focus on. She took a very deep breath put her chin to her chest and pushed for all she was worth.

"Now blow a feather with short breaths out and just pant. We don't want the baby to come out too quickly now do we!" The doctor said, trying to calm her down. I could feel her grip tightening on my hand and knew that there was another pain coming. I hoped this wasn't going to go on for too long I needed both my hands. The pain grew more intense and chin to chest she pushed and pushed for all she was worth. A tiny sound of a new life drawing breath and making their sound for the first time was music to my ears. After a long nine and three quarter hours if pain and sweat and yes blood! Baby Luis was born. My Saskia's baby had finally made an appearance.

The baby was screaming for all he was worth, a wriggling purple, bloodstained, bundle of scrawny arms and legs; yet such a beautiful sight. How blessed I was to have witnessed the miracle of life at its very beginning. OH MY GOD, a tiny little human being. He was immaculate, so very perfect. After they checked him out they handed him straight to me wrapped in a white towel. "Here is your son daddy" the nurse said as she laid him in my arms. Oh my! Is that what they thought? I could not speak. I was numb. I had just seen this little man born. It was quite amazing and there he was in my arms. He had a head full of dark wet hair and twinkling dark eyes. He was perfect.

Saskia looked out of it and so very tired. It had been a long nine months for her. They washed Saskia all over and cleaned her up while all the time I held her new son. He weighed all of 5 pound and 3 ounces. After the nurses had finished with Saskia and she looked a bit better than she had done in the last few hours she said to me

"Thank you Christian for being there for us. I am calling him Luis." I was extremely happy about this as my middle name was Luis. I leaned across and handed her Luis for some bonding time with his mum and so that he could be fed. He took immediately to the breast as if he had been doing it all his life. I watched as Saskia leant into the role of a doting mother. It made a change to see her like this she was usually off her face. This was beautiful to watch, a woman becoming a mother.

"Should I call anyone Sask?" I asked as she began to wind him.

"Like who Christian?" she queried.

"Erm… your mum? Maybe his father?......" I replied.

"NO! Thank you hunny – they will find out soon enough and they will see Luis in due time" She said very sure of herself. I couldn't go against her wishes so I didn't call anybody. She had to spend one night in hospital just so that both she and Luis could relax after their ordeal. She had done so well and there were no complications and for her first baby the staff said she did very well.

"I am just going out for a smoke I wont be too long I promise" I said to her as I turned to walk away.

"OK" she said looking absolutely shattered. I stood at the doorway and watched as Saskia held her baby and mother and son fixed gazes and began the bonding process. I would leave now and pay my dues to the staff for their help, for without them to help bring baby Luis into this world I would have panicked. I wondered as I watched what was his future going to be like. What events did the world have in store for him? All I knew was that I would do the best I could for him and give him everything he should have in life.

Luis was taking his milk and filling up his nappies just right! Saskia finally started settling down to sleep and I stayed by Luis and her all night. I was allowed to sleep over in the chair besides them. I shut the curtains and turned off the lights. I covered up Saskia all snug and warm. She looked relaxed and content. I walked over to the little cot besides her bed. He slept so soundly too. WOW so tiny, so fragile. It was hard to imagine this tiny little bundle all screwed up inside Saskia's tummy kicking her from the inside. What a miracle! He had won my heart already. I stroked his hair very softly and as gentle as I could. He was content too. He looked like his mum; the blonde hair was the same. Still I could only relate to his mother, I had no clue as to who his father was. I had already decided I was going to be the entire dad he needed. I was going to give him the world. I guess I thought back to my past that moment, where was my dad, why didn't I have a dad who was there for me and close to me? Luis was NOT going to ever feel that way I did and I vowed I would never let him down.

On our return home we got plenty of looks as we stepped out of the car baby in car seat and making our way to the front door. You could see people from the village waiting at the bottom of the short drive behind the wrought iron fencing look at us, Saskia, the baby and me when we came back to the village. They didn't know what to think half the time and most assumed he was my baby and I didn't give a shit if that's what they thought, I wanted people to think he had a dad. I decided in my heart to stand by Saskia and help her both emotionally and financially. I liked playing Daddy but I had no idea about the responsibility that was to come and just how hard it was going to be.

CHAPTER 8

THAT MAN

E very Friday night I noticed a guy coming into the bar on what appeared to be a regular basis always at 10pm. I would be on stage dancing but I took everything in. Spyros played the devoted slave and gave him everything he wanted. He would kiss the guys hand and drop a bow sort of, this was a sign of respect I could tell. A drink would be ready for him and a table right in the middle so he could get a good view of what was happening on stage. His table, round with a white table cloth, a red rose in the vase sitting proudly in the centre. After a while I began to think about this man. He was tall and very classically dressed a coat around his shoulders and gold on his hands and wrists. He was always impeccably dressed in a black or navy Armani suit, his shoes beautifully shined, and his hair immaculate with not a hair out of place this man was something truly special, it was obvious that he had the money to keep his grooming regime up. The same time every week he would come in without fail and just sit and watch me and then once my spot had finished he would get up and leave. He never seemed to pay for anything and was treated like some kind of royalty. I was going to make it my business to find out who he was. Questions were going around in my head such as "who the fuck was he?" Why was he so important? Why was he watching me? Why leave so abruptly and not wait for any of the others to take their turn? In the dressing room it began to get a bit bitchy with questions being fired at me about him. How the hell did I know! I wasn't anyone special or was I!?

I began to look out for him and in the meantime I practiced every day and endeavoured to improve my performance. I watched the clock and got nervous when he arrived, my heart pumping. I was finding him very attractive and appealing. Each week there he would be just there to watch me week after week after week.

One Friday night I wasn't feeling too good and didn't feel like dancing so I asked Spyros if I could help behind the bar. He agreed. At the usual time the guy with no name walked in and looked toward the stage, he noticed I wasn't there and looked around and found me behind the bar, so what does he do? Sits at the bar all night and doesn't use his table. One of the girls working with me made him his usual drink and then brought down to me a shot of vodka.

"It's from the guy down there Chris" She said

I held the glass up to say thank you and as I caught his face he had the most gorgeous smile I had ever seen.

"Yamass!" He called and we downed our shots together looking at each other.

That clinched it. This guy was certainly interested in me and I was fast becoming interested in him and intrigued too.

His name was Niko. I found out his name from the girl who gave me the shot. After we drank the vodka shot he made his way over to the bar. God he was really a good looking man.

"Not dancing tonight?" he asked speaking in a very heavy Greek accent. I shook my head feeling embarrassed and replied

"No. But thank you for the drink" These were the first words I had uttered to him and he could tell I had a speech impediment from my disjointed words. He stayed longer than his normal 30 minutes and propped up the bar for the rest of the evening. He could see I was working and was very professional about it. He watched me as I worked and gave me sideways glances and smiles. When my shift had finished I began to get ready to leave and he asked

"Why don't you come and join me for a drink?" Well, who was I to say no.

I could see from the looks that Spyro was giving me he was a little jealous and not very happy with me. Still it wasn't my fault if the man wanted to have a drink with me. After all wasn't that what we were employed to do? Look after the customers. Anyway, I had been watching him for a long time now and at last I was getting a chance to find out who this man was. I draped my jacket over the back of the stool I was guided to and sat beside him.

"Where did you learn to dance so well?" He asked.

"I have been in love with dancing from a very young age" I said to him.

"You are very good at it" he said with a laugh which made me smile and blush!!

He told me he was born on the island, was 46 years old and single. I had an idea that he may be gay, well he must be, it wouldn't be normal for a straight guy coming in and watching me dance and strip and then walk out when my time was done would it! He was a business man and travelled a great deal to many different countries. He didn't really say what it was about, his business; he would just call it "family business". He was dreamy looking and very confident. He looked at his watch and said

"Erm! Christian I really do have to go now but I was wondering if maybe I could take you out sometime."

Well I HAD to smile then OH MY GOD he was asking me out! ME! What did he want with me I was just a dancer at a club? I wanted more but was I ever going to get it? Well I had to smile then and thought to myself OH MY GOD! He was asking ME out – he WAS a poof! – Whey hey!!!! It was all my birthdays come early! I was rather nervous too as I had never been out with a man before. I mean I had been out with guys, like my own age, but not a MAN and certainly not one as gorgeous as he was and as refined.

"Let's say I pick you up from here tomorrow night at about 10pm? Is that ok with you?"

"Yes! Of course! 10pm sounds great!" I replied without even thinking too long about it. He slung his drink down his throat stood up and put his hands on my shoulders kissing me on each cheek

"Tomorrow then?" I nodded and he walked out of the bar.

I stood there for a while, in a little shock, numb from being touched with such excitement I had never known before. I wanted to run round the bar kissing everyone and laughing. I had a date! A REAL DATE!!! On my way home all I could think about was Niko and when I would be seeing him tomorrow night. I had visions of his smile, the way his teeth glistened and how they were immaculately straight and the way his goatee fitted his masculine jaw line perfectly. He was perfect, at least in my eyes he was. How was I going to sleep that night I did not know, he was all I could think of. How was I going to go into work do my set and then be "normal" afterwards when he arrived at 10pm. Jesus!!! I didn't want to go to work now I had met him personally; I was a little embarrassed about taking my clothes off and dancing now. I went to bed thinking about nothing but him. I tossed and turned for what seemed like hours. What should I wear? How should I behave? This was proving to be a long night! He excited me like no other had done before and he brought alive my hormones. I took matters into my own hand, if you get my drift and I wouldn't be surprised if the whole island heard me screaming his name "NIKO!!!!!!!!!!"

The morning soon came and I was lying in bed looking up at the ceiling smiling – yes just smiling, I wore myself out the night before! I grabbed a shower and ate some breakfast and made a start on the household chores. Saskia would be visiting that afternoon too so I wanted it to be pristine for her visit, we would have some laughs together and she had loads of gossip on what was happening to everyone. I knew she would be pissed at the thought of me going on a date, but I was not going to turn this date with Niko down in a lifetime! I had a neat shave to make my goatee look perfect. I ironed a crisp white shirt to wear with my denims – Yes I was going to keep my "old faithfuls" on, they were my lucky jeans. I packed a bag with some deodorant, hair gel along with toothbrush and toothpaste. Well! I would be meeting him after my slot in Adonis so I would need freshening up, and as I took great pride in my appearance I wanted to look and smell just right for him! Saskia arrived and we chatted and had drinks together, she didn't look too well but she told me she was meeting up with some guy to go to the cinema and watch a film. I was pleased for her and wished her luck for her date and she wished me the same for mine, but she made it known how she disapproved of the age gap.

"Bollocks!" I said to her "Age is only a number!"

Work went rather fast that night, my heart pumping with the expectation of what was to come later that evening. I danced my spot and ripped off my clothes a lot faster than I had ever done. I just wanted the work time to end and move on to the latter part of the evening with Niko. I wanted to be ready on time as he didn't strike me as being the sort of person to hang around waiting and he struck me as being the guy who always got what he wanted when he wanted. I knew he would look stunning and I wanted to please him so I paid particular attention to my grooming that evening.

My session for the evening was over and I showered in the dressing room, showers were provided for the employees use as dancing for hours on end in a smoke filled club it was essential that we were clean and tidy after work as well as being made up for work.

I looked at the clock on the dressing room wall, the time, ten minutes to ten. I was now showered and smelling good. I walked out of the dressing room and said my hello's etc to the punters watching the next turn. I made my way to the bar with a knot in my stomach. I asked for a brandy, as I handed the barman my money to pay and the dulcet tones of greasy man Spyro rang in my ear.

"Have it on me Christian" he said with a booming voice and a dirty grin on his face. I knew he wanted me but I had set my sights high and he certainly wasn't even on the radar as someone I would want to be with. He was just my boss and that was the way it was going to stay. The hustle and bustle of the bar ceased for a second, I looked up and there he was! My eyes were straight on him looking him up and down. How handsome he was, immaculate from top to toe and I was going on a date with him. Me! Little Christian, the deaf boy and local celebrity, from the village next door, the one they said would never amount to anything because of my disability. He was absolutely stunning. He was wearing Jeans, which was not like him from what I had seen so far, and a white shirt! We could almost be twins! He looked gorgeous and a man after my own heart. Something I hadn't noticed before, he had an earring in his ear and this really suited him.

"Another large brandy Christian?" Niko asked winking at the barman serving.

We smiled at each other downed our brandies and left. Outside was a huge fuck off car with its own driver – Jesus was this a dream or what!? This sort of thing just did not happen to me. We went to an expensive restaurant approximately 30 miles from my village, a place I had only heard of but had never been to. We had the most perfect meal and drank brandies like they were going out of fashion!! We laughed and we communicated. He was very interested in my dancing and amazed at my disability. He asked a lot about my family too and what was my home like. I told him I could not complain, that I had been able to pay my way and did the best I could.

"You are a sweet boy Christian" He said touching my hand tenderly and talking to me. I certainly knew then that he was gay. The evening came to an end and we both skipped desert, I think we had too much brandy! He asked for the bill and the manager appeared.

"With compliments Niko!" He said kissing his hand. For fuck sake that was certainly a sight to see. Have your meals for free and I will kiss your hand too – what for eating it!? We gathered our coats and got back into the car which was still waiting outside for us. I was even more intrigued by this time. He took me home in his car and dropped me off outside. I had visions of Mama looking out of the window wanting to know where I had been. He looked at me

"Thank you for a wonderful evening Christian" he said looking at every inch of my face.

"Thank you Niko I had a blast too" I replied. He leant into me and brushed my cheek with the back of his hand and pulled my face towards him kissing me tenderly on the lips. Our lips were closed but I could tell he wanted more. I pulled away slightly relieving some of the pressure I was feeling. He looked at me deep into my eyes

"Let me see you again Christian?"

"Oh! Yes, yes!" Was my reply and we both laughed. He said he would contact me soon. I left the car and watched him drive away. Feeling contented and happy with the proceedings of the evening I went into the house calm and happy.

I continued to work in Adonis and Niko constantly came in to watch and run his rituals. He certainly only had eyes for me. Presents started arriving not just at work but at home too. Consisting of clothes, underwear, flowers, chocolates and even cigarettes, they were gifts I had never received in such abundance before. We met after work 3 nights a week and we would go out to eat, watch a film, bowling drinking and sometimes just go for a walk along the shore. We would take slow walks hand in hand in the moonlight catching the ripples of the sea on our feet. We would sit and cuddle for hours on the beach and just watch the waves rush up the shore rippling over the tiny crustaceans making the homes in the sand.

"Christian? I have very strong feelings for you and I would like to see more of you." He said one night sitting on the blanket on the sand. I smiled at him an impish smile with eyes twinkling. God! I was crazy about him and thought there was no other to match this wonderful, loving man. He was all I thought about day and night. He wanted me to make a commitment to him to date seriously.

"I would like that very much Niko" and I hugged him close taking in the wafting smell of his aftershave. Inside I was as excited as a child being given a new present. I felt as if I was 15 again.

One evening we were taking our normal walk along the beach and he turned to me and said

"Christian? I have something to show you. I do hope you are going to like it" I half expected him to pull a ring out of his pocket or something, but we continued walking. He moved behind me and put his hands over my eyes. I wondered what it was he had in store for me.

"Trust me Christian, let me lead you to your present" he said as he guided me a bit further down the beach. I put my arms out to feel my way, not wanting to bang into anything or trip and make a complete fool of myself. I came to a stop and felt with my hands, the metal was cold and thin.

"Where are you taking me Niko?" I asked.

"Open your eyes and tell me what you think" he asked dropping his hands slowly. I was standing at the entrance of a property, I didn't get it?

"What's this Niko?" I asked looking at the house and then at him.

"It's our new house" he replied with the biggest grin on his face I had seen to date.

"Ours!?" I asked. "Yes Christian. I want you to move in with me and be my proper partner."

This was a stunning house, absolutely stunning. I was a little speechless to say the least. He unlocked the gates and we walked up the drive. He went on to explain to me that he had bought the house sometime ago as an investment but since he had met me he thought it was perfect for us to live. Close to all that I had known and grown up around it was walking distance to my family and friends. Mama's house was big, but this was enormous. It was a huge two storey house with white and cream walls, marble stairways and marble floors. The beach ran up to the edge of the property and was shielded from the road by a hill for our privacy. It had been built from scratch using the plans that Niko had devised. It was eye catching. In the reception area of the house there was a massive half circle stairway wrapped around a fountain with a small pool in the middle of the hall. It was wall to wall marble floors. It was like something I had seen in a film or read about in a book, it was luxurious. The living room was enormous. It had burnished oak floors and almost floor to ceiling arched windows. With spectacular ocean views this spacious living room was light and bright but had a cosy fireplace too.

Niko had added a den for me to do with what I chose. Here I could entertain my friends and chill out. It had a pool table in the centre and games machines, some of which were modern but many more were vintage such as the pool cues. There were pinball machines, a jukebox, a television, stereo and a soft cushioned floor, with mirrors all around. This was a dream. It also had a fully fitted optic bar with many different brands of brandy and vodka. There were three leather sofas all white and situated around a huge glass coffee table adorned with one candle and a bowl of fresh fruit. I had never seen such elaborate tastes. There was also to the side was a room housing exercise equipment, a punching bag, multi gyms, running machines, so that we could all keep up our exercise regime. The gourmet kitchen had lots of counter space with granite worktops, recessed lighting and stainless steel appliances. Our room was amazing. Niko called it the master bedroom. The room had its own marble fireplace white shag pile carpet. The bed stretched out before you, a four poster with elaborate drapes around it and beautiful silk bedding. Attached to this room was an en suite bathroom adorned with gold taps, a Jacuzzi tub with marble tile. There was a separate shower cubicle big enough to walk in and large enough to take at least two if not more people. The tub was round and rather large. You could fit at least four people in it. There were mirrors everywhere; Niko certainly did like the opulent look. In the room itself along one wall there were massive closets all mirrored. What were all these mirrors here for I wondered? The house had five bedrooms all decorated to the most extravagant designs. This house wreaked money and this was to become my home. How long for, one did not know; but if this was my home for the rest of my life I was not complaining.

It was a Friday night, I had my rucksack packed with just a few items of clothing, some of my trophies my tapes and cd collection. Niko had told me I wouldn't need much. "Kids!" Mama shouted up the stairs. "Your dinner is ready, please come down and eat" I became a bit anxious as I knew this was going to be the time I would have to tell the family I was moving out to live with Niko. I made my way down the staircase and before my eyes was a sumptuous array of foods. Mama truly did excel herself when it came to meal times. It looked like a banquet. We all gathered around the table and we held hands as Mama blessed our meal. This was the time of day when we all gathered and discussed our goings on for the day. There was Riki, Mama, Teresa and TJ. One person was missing, Toni, he didn't like the tradition we had to all gather together, but Mama was right this was the time of day we all gathered to be a family. All of us having busy lives, everyone looked forward to it, except Toni! But then Mama liked it that way as whenever he was there somehow there always seemed to be a row. He didn't like us I don't think; all he wanted was Mama to be his slave. We didn't like the way he treated Mama and TJ would stand up to him. After we completed our meal I left the table and went to the lounge to sit and relax and have a smoke. I lit up a joint I had prepared earlier and before I got the chance to light it properly and start to smoke it there was a thud! Right across the back of my head. She hated me smoking at the best of times but to light up a joint in front of Mama thinking I was all grown up was not a good idea. I should have known better, I knew her feelings on that kind of thing. I put the joint down and lit a cigarette instead.

"Mama! All of you – I have something to tell you would you please come and sit with me." I called in a rather serious way.

"OH! MY GOD Mama! He is pregnant!" TJ shouted with a grin on his face. He always took the piss out of me because of me being gay.

"Shut up!" Mama yelled getting everyone's attention. "Shush kids listen to Christian please." Thanks to Mama I now had everyone's attention.

"OK you guys! Well – you know I have been seriously dating somebody for a while now – well I am moving out" The room went silent for what seemed a life time but was probably only a few seconds, then the atmosphere was cut in two by the shriek of

"YES! YES! YES! I get the bathroom longer now!!!!!!!!!!" Everyone looked towards Teresa and suddenly she felt like a naughty schoolgirl sitting the corner sporting a dunce's cap! Ricky and TJ didn't say anything they didn't normally anyway so I didn't expect much of a reaction. Everyone just sat there waiting for Mama's reaction

"Sorry!" Teresa gingerly said a little embarrassed. The focus then went from Teresa to me and I now knew how Teresa felt in those few preceding minutes. Mama sat down her legs together her hands in her lap and looked a white as a sheep, the golden olive glow of her skin turned ashen.

"Mama?" I softly spoke leaning in to take her hand to let her know that everything was alright. Her eyes, dark with something I had never seen before, her grip getting tighter and tighter as the blood surged round her veins, all of a sudden she jumped up letting go of my hand.

"NO! NO! No way Christian!" she yelled at me crossing her self for all she was worth. Praying to God in her rantings. She was very hurt. This was a sight I hoped I would never hear or see.

"Oh Mama! Please let me explain." She grabbed hold of me by the shoulders tears running like rivulets down her face. She looked broken and I had done that. I had ruined her life I could tell. But why would she take this so bad I asked myself. She doesn't really know Niko.

"You have not known each other very long Christian!"

"How can you just go and live with him? Give your life and everything you are? Please Christian I beg of you please don't do this" She pleaded with me almost on her knees, but I took a strong hold of her and helped her to her seat. This was a major decision I had made but I did not in any way think that Mama, who had always let me make my own choices as long as I obeyed her, would have taken it so hard.

"Christian, my baby, if you were with this person for a long time and we all knew him really well, I would be so happy for you. But we don't know him, we don't even know his name, we have never met him. I tell you Christian I worry for you my angel"

"Its all wrong" she said" She had calmed down after the initial shock and I began to explain to her softly.

"I have made my mind up Mama, I am going." I replied. I had totally fucked up the dinner but what was I to do?" Teresa was the only one who seemed excited and happy for me.

"Do what you have to Christian. I will always be your sister," She said with a smile that told me I knew she meant every word. These were pleasing words to hear. I felt for Mama but I felt that after she had sat down and taken it all in she would understand that I am not the lost little deaf boy anymore. I was growing up and I had to go out on my own one day so why not now, with someone who worshipped the ground I walked on and I had everything my heart could desire. Once she got to know him she would be fine to see that someone so powerful was taking good care of me and loved me. I knew once she saw the house she would fall in love with it and be happy for Niko and me.

The morning came and I arose in a wonderful ebullient mood. All my dreams were coming true. I had become an earning dancer and I had found someone I could really see me spending the rest of my life with. I heard a car draw up outside so I leapt out of bed and went to the window. Lo and behold he was entering Mamas territory in classical style, in only the way Niko knew how.

"WOW!!!!!!!!" Teresa screamed in such a high pitched sound that only dogs should be able to hear. "He must be loaded" She added.

"Right! That's me I guess!" I had chucked some clothes on while the entire debacle was going on outside. Usual trademark, jeans, t-shirt, trainers and not forgetting my sunglasses. I grabbed my bag on the way out the door, ran down the stairs and out to the car. I put my bag in the car and bade my farewells. By the time I got there Mama had disappeared and was nowhere to be seen. I searched and searched but time was pressing on and I had to go. I wasn't going far and I would still be able to see them every day. But I guess in Mama's eyes she was watching her broken winged bird fly to a new nest. Teresa hugged and kissed me and wished me well. Riki shook my hand and gave a look which said to me to be careful and he would be there if I had a problem. TJ looked at me as I outstretched my arms to him, turned his back and walked away.

"Oh Well!" I thought everything will work out fine just give a few days to let the dust settle and we will be ok. But I do wish Mama had come out just before I got in the car and said good luck at least. She didn't appear so I got in the car and kissed Niko and then off we went. This would be the first time I had left home and I didn't want to leave with Mama so down.

What I found really strange was when we first looked at the house, the very first time; I noticed coat hooks behind the bathroom door holding two robes. They were white and very comfy looking but they both already had a motif on the breast pocket. Part was my initials and part was Niko's. The bath towels were matching too; it appeared as if I had been living there for awhile. The place had been prepared for me. What would he have done if I had said no! Niko had spared no expense in furnishing the house and making it feel like home to me. The opulence was astounding.

After the first month went by I awoke to find a note pinned to Niko's pillow it read *"To my darling Christian, for you on our one month anniversary love Niko. P.S. Look under the pillow"* I lifted the pillow so fast and underneath were some shiny new KEYS!!!! Car keys at that. I fell over my own legs trying to put on my jeans; I was so excited I couldn't wait to see my gift. I flew down the stairs missing the last three and bare foot ran to the front door. There stood before me none other than an Audi in ice silver. Its top speed kicked a mere 155 mph. Wow! I looked inside and it had black and pink interior. I had to smile at the pink; he had remembered one of my favourite colours was pink. It even had a rear view parking camera and much more exciting a Bang & Olufsen sound system. She was immaculate. The number plate read "BOY 1". All the legal documents were sitting on the passenger seat. The car ownership, breakdown cover and insurance documents were in an envelope which I put in the glove compartment. I just wanted to burn this baby. WOW!!!!! I had my own car and what a beauty!!!!!!.

That night we walked down to the beach where our favourite little bay was. It was situated just outside of sight of the world going by. I stood by the edge of the water and lifted off my shirt, threw it to one side so that it wouldn't get wet and my denims followed.

"Come Niko. Come to me" I said to him and put out my hands, he lifted off his top and his trousers came off next, he kicked off his shoes and socks and threw them all with mine. He put out his hands and walked towards me. We held hands and I backed up into the water he went with me and then we knelt down in the cool night water, the stars shining above our heads twinkling like the lights you get on a Christmas tree that blink on and off.

We kissed and fondled each other until we could no longer control our urges. It was beautiful making love under the stars in this heavenly place, with the most gorgeous man I had ever met, it was our special place and we had made this bay a place of sanctuary for both of us. We moaned and groaned together as our bodies connected. Our kisses were like little electric shocks racing through my body. Our hearts beating fast and the blood surging round my body filled me with an urgency I could not explain. I wanted him so bad I ached for him. All we had together until now was just the dreams of a small boy, but now the way he was touching me and the way my skin rippled at his touch was driving me insane. I HAD to have him As he kissed me I turned my body and he traced my turn with his tongue, sliding up my neck to my ear and little nibbles along the lobe of my ear only heated me up more. He had his hands on my shoulders squeezing them each squeeze another reassurance that we were making wonderful love together. He kissed along my shoulders to the nape of my neck I dropped my head back submitting to his touch. He moved his hands slowly down my arms holding my hands in his and meeting them at the front of me. Holding my hands with his left hand he took his right hand and traced up my arm to my shoulder across my neck and down my spine, I started to lean over urging him to press a little harder as the ecstasy started to fill me. I leant right over the jetty in front of me my legs spread. I looked behind me and saw the excitement that Niko possessed. We smiled and he took himself in his manly hand and found the entrance to what I could only describe as pleasure beyond measure. The atmosphere between us was electric and as Niko just went for it faster and faster and deeper and deeper I too used my hand faster and faster and harder and harder. This was the most enjoyable union I had had in a very long time if ever!

Our bodies spent we stayed in the water and swam about for a while meeting occasionally for a peck and a knowing glance between us. After a short while and beginning to feel the chill in the night air we strolled hand in hand along the path back to our haven of solitude Paradisia.

Our six month anniversary came along really fast. It had been the best six months I had experienced in a very long time. We spent all morning swimming together in our pool. We drank champagne and he did his white powder whilst I rolled up a spliff and chilled leaning back against the edge of the pool.

"Christian! I bought you something really special for today but I couldn't wrap it up and bring it to you, you are going to have to come to me and see it" He said laughing. I kissed him all over his face gratefully giggling. We dressed casually and took a stroll down the high street. People would nod their heads and wave to us as we walked by holding hands. Nobody said anything about us holding hands and they wouldn't have dared judge Niko anyway. I felt safe in this world. We got to a place in the high street that was quite a busy part. Niko took my hand and turned me to face something in front of us. OH MY LORD!!!!!!! I thought "What on earth is it?" I asked myself. The sign in front of me read "CHRISTIANS" in big bold black letters. It was situated just to the left of the filling station and stood out amongst all the other small buildings around it. I looked at Niko with tears in my eyes and my heart pumping. He gave me the keys. I undid the locks and opened the door gingerly. What would be inside? I lifted my head as I entered the door. I took a huge gasp "WOW!" I screeched; it was HUGE! It was unique and very tastefully decorated. On both sides of the walls were floor to ceiling mirrors. There was an office where I could see the entire goings on via the CCTV cameras that had been put in various places. This was just to make sure that nobody cut in on his family business. The office was quite luxurious and had an en suite bathroom with changing facilities and a wet room whose shelves were adorned with no end of oils and foams, soap and gels, clean towels soft and white and bathrobes for those who needed them. It was just like Niko IMMACULATE!

On the other side of the club there were the male and female changing rooms with showers and toilets. All were colour coordinated and fitted to the highest specifications. What else would I expect from Niko? When it came to elaborate décor Niko was the king and adapted every space for its main occupier. Outside there was ample parking with two designated places for staff. This was way beyond anything I had ever seen before or could dream of. The floors all lay to wood and highly polished. Adorning the walls at specific measurements were some of the most beautiful scenery in Corfu. It had its own kitchen area where you could get drinks and some food. The deeds and all the relevant paperwork were safely and meticulously filed all bound in a folder laid on the desk. Niko didn't miss a thing!

By the entry doors stood a huge oak desk. I guessed this would be the reception area and where enquiries could be answered.

"I will work this really hard Niko; I want to make you proud of me!" I said to him as I was taking every inch in. I had to sort out opening times and sort out our dance classes, but I knew it wouldn't take long to get the place up and running. The islands first properly equipped dance classes. I was able to afford to hire a fulltime receptionist and two dance teachers with the budget Niko had allowed me. I would plan a big open evening and combine it with a launch party. "CHRISTIANS" had hit sunny Corfu. Were they ready for what was about to be unleashed on them? I don't think so!

The open evening came and we had such a wonderful time. Niko was amazing with his support and encouragement to me. I asked him to officially open "CHRISTIANS". A crowd gathered outside and Niko took hold of the gold scissors and cut the beautiful red ribbon. "I Niko declare this dance school officially open". At least someone had faith in me and what I could achieve. It was my plan, or rather one of them, to open up a string of dance schools like "CHRISTIANS". I knew that I would be a success as long as I had Niko by my side.

There were several genres of dance that I enjoyed but my favourite was Latin. This was one of the lessons I would give in my dance school. Many different types of people came to "CHRISTIANS"; there were those who had money and those who didn't. Coming from the background I did I could totally understand how hard it was for some people. I built up a wardrobe of clothes for the pupils to use if the could not afford their own. I instilled in my students the need to not be embarrassed when dancing in front of others. To stand tall and be proud of who they were. If I could do it then they could too and I was not going to let any one of them fail. I love teaching and hopefully I will still be doing it when I get older. When I was teaching I could hear Ms Buddana urging me on, tapping her stick. When I say hear, I know I am deaf and she is dead but with the echoing sound in the studio I was able to hear after a fashion and she was always there in spirit watching me.

Whenever somebody new came to my studio they were welcomed by me and they shook my hand out of respect. If you have never been to a dance studio before it can be quite intimidating and the student can feel completely out of their depth. I have a knack of reading people and I soon learnt which pairs I could make up when the class had to work on the pas de deux. Everyone was friendly and there weren't any snobs in there. Every person was there to help someone else. While we were learning a dance the students would all stand in front of the mirrors and watch each other try and do the steps, I was at the front and by miming the words to the song I managed to get the students to follow me. I had fun when I had "CHRISTIANS", I loved to teach people to dance and see how much they progressed over time. The majority of my lessons were 40 minutes long, but there would be times when I just didn't want to stop and I would dance for three hours. The people there had seen me grow from an uncomfortable, shy, deaf boy who fought everyone he could, to a confident dance teacher and a mild mannered man who had no shame in the fact that he was gay. I have not thought about the dance lessons I had and Ms Buddana for many years. They were wonderful memories from a near perfect time in my life. It was at the time when music became the life force I know it as today. I define my life through Music and dance. The classes were mixed and probably my best friend in the world was Saskia, she used to have lessons here too. There were so many difficult things in my life but dance came easy to me and that was when I was at my happiest and felt very safe.

CHAPTER 9

THE MIRACLE OF SOUND

As you will have already been noted, I was born deaf. I could only lip read and learn to write and this was taught to me by Mama. As the years progressed there were advances in scientific research and an implant was developed to put behind the ear which would hopefully enable a person to "hear". Mama had kept up with all the new things coming out so that when something did eventually turn up if it was not too expensive maybe I would be able to have one.

For those of you who don't know what this is I will try to explain it. A cochlear implant is a small electronic device that can help to provide a sense of sound to a person who is profoundly deaf or severely hard-of-hearing. The implant sits behind the ear and a second portion is then surgically placed under the skin. Originally, cochlear implants were limited to the most severely deaf, but the criteria had loosened over the years. I knew that based on my last hearing test results, I would probably qualify.

An implant does not restore normal hearing. Instead, it can give a deaf person a useful representation of sounds in the environment and help him or her to understand speech.

A cochlear implant is very different from a hearing aid. Hearing aids amplify sounds so they may be detected by damaged ears. Cochlear implants bypass damaged portions of the ear and directly stimulate the auditory nerve. Signals generated by the implant are sent by way of the auditory nerve to the brain, which recognizes the signals as sound. Hearing through an implant is different from normal hearing and takes time to learn or relearn. However, it allowed me to recognize warning signals, understand other sounds in the environment, and enjoy a conversation in person or by telephone. It brought a whole new way of life to me. I had been raised to wear a hearing aid and it was really quite an ugly piece of equipment. I used to leave it in places hoping mama would not realize I did not have it on but Mama used to shout at me

"If it can make you hear traffic, then it's important to wear it". I guess she was right.

I had been stripping for long enough to have saved privately for this operation and the occasional private party dance helped but Niko in the end funded it all. He said I had strived so hard to save money and worked really hard for it he wanted to give me this gift.

I hadn't lived very long at Paradisia when I was packing a case and going to stay elsewhere but not just anywhere. I had my own private room in a very elite private clinic and it was there I had my implant. Previously I had to go to the Ear, Nose, and

Throat specialist. He was the one who would review my test results, order additional tests, and refer me to a cochlear implant program. He agreed that I was probably a good candidate and we would move forward. He ordered a CAT scan to determine if my cochlea was in adequate enough shape for an implant. I had the scan done .The ENT reviewed the scan, and referred me to the private clinic. I felt Niko just told them at no matter what cost give him the best you can. I had to stay in the clinic for two days after the surgery. I think the time went really fast in there and I slept a lot of the time to be pain free. Niko was by my side constantly – well every time I opened my eyes he was there. I had slight dizziness but that was all. They warn you of things like infection and worst facial problems. I had got through it ok it seemed. Three weeks after the surgical wound healed I returned to the implant clinic to be fitted with the external parts of the device (the speech processor, microphone, and transmitter). A clinician tunes the speech processor and sets levels of stimulation for each electrode, from soft to loud. I was then trained in how to interpret the sounds heard through the device. Apparently the length of the training varied from days to years, depending on how well the person can interpret the sounds heard through the device. From the very beginning I was hearing things quite differently. I realized that I missed experiencing sound. Another reason pushing me towards this implant were a desire to hear my boyfriend speak, to cut down the frustrations I had in communication with hearing people, and to improve my personal safety. Once I thought that an implant was like a hearing aid. All I knew were "they cut a hole in your head" and I freaked out!!

New sounds were amazing to me. To hear running water that was so nice. Music my passion was so much clearer. I think I even started to hear Niko snore which he denied! Who would have ever thought I would be the one turning the music down but some days the headaches were so bad I just could not concentrate on anything. It took a time to settle and work properly and I took some time to recognize different new sounds but all the same it was an amazing device that was opening new doors to me. WOW!! Didn't Yankees speak so different, with this thing now I could hear different accents also and it was fun trying to mimic them and I was quite good at that.

As a deaf child I should have been in close contact with the doctors and deaf community. The doctors will tell you not to teach your child sign language because it is a crutch, well they are wrong. Teaching your child sign language will help them to communicate better without getting frustrated that they cannot speak or get their point across. I was grateful that Mama had taken the patience and time to teach me to speak a little.

If you are deaf you can go to school you can get a job you can achieve anything a hearing person can. Being deaf is not an embarrassment, and does not mean that you are not normal. It means you cherish life and instead of hearing with your ears you hear visually. The deaf community was incredible they would tell you the truth, they were not one-sided, and they were honest. I would never forget what I endured growing up as a deaf child. I went without a lot in some ways but was given so much more in others.

Music sounded wonderful, I could pick up the sounds of different instruments and I totally fell in love with the saxophone and the piano. I always thought the piano sounded like raindrops and I was not far wrong there, for when my hearing was installed it was as I thought, each tinkle on they keys a pitter patter of raindrops on a window. The telephone took some getting used to and I was soon brave enough to make and receive calls myself. The first few calls were hilarious as I kept on saying words wrong and getting everything back to front. This implant truly had given me a new lease of life and I would be ever grateful for that. Having a disability was always a fight. It was a constant battle to be heard and a fight for independence. I was often spoken to as a child and this made me feel very insecure and frustrated as I so wanted to be understood but was incapable of that until the cochlea implant. I was deaf not thick and I soon grew short tempered over people's attitudes to me and the way they would sometimes exclude me, maybe not purposefully, but nevertheless they did. I had been raised with three languages going on in the house; Greek, English and sign language. But now I could hear those languages, I used my lip reading as a guide and within a short space of time had picked up quite a few words and had learned to speak. I did have some therapy to help me and I was very grateful for the care and attention the therapists gave me. I wondered if I would hear the music the same as I did before I had my implant, however, after a while it was a double blessing to be able to still feel the rhythm but also to hear the different notes and this I hoped would make me a better dancer, if that was possible! To hear the hustle and bustle of children's conversations and the many different sounds of the market, hearing the vendors before you see them. To hear the church's bells, the birds singing. I had appreciated everything I had seen and felt before but now my world had opened up just like the skies clearing their way so that the sun could shine through. The different things that the children came out with and the chuckles in response to things and were a joy to see and more importantly to hear!

Luis had the cutest accent; he didn't sound Greek very much just well spoken, what someone might judge as being "posh"! The more sounds I heard the quicker I learnt. Languages, accents, warning noises, music, animals and even the sea and weather changes held an audible noise, to hear was totally amazing!!!

Niko's voice was very heavily accented unlike mine. Hearing me was so funny at times though and I would make people scream with laughter when I mimicked others. Laughter was a beautiful sound and I would thank Niko every day for what he had done and he knew I had received a miracle and he always told me that I had deserved it. I would never forget what he had done for me as I had felt a bit like an outcast most of my life and hearing people couldn't understand how I felt. I felt that this procedure should be available to all hearing impaired people even if they were poor. This truly was a miracle and everyone should be able to hear. This bodes the question is hearing a luxury or a necessity.

My speech rapidly improved and through this I found a new confidence. Even though I had built up a certain amount of confidence through dancing and having things happen to me throughout my life, I was still pretty insecure because I was unable to hear. I would feel left out of conversations and permanently watching peoples lips became a headache. Some signed to me but this was generally the family which restricted my social life. The only time I really felt free was when I would dance and feel the vibrations now those vibrations were enhanced by the magical sound of music. It was a little scary at first but I soon came to embrace what was happening in my world.

CHAPTER 10

GOOD TIMES TURN

From the beginning of my time with Niko he demonstrated a fetish for washing me or trying to keep me clean. He liked everything immaculate and orderly to the point of it being an obsession. At first it seemed like a fetish, but the need to be clean became stronger and stronger as time went on. It was as if he found something dirty about me and needed to wash the dirt away. He became moody and angry and much more obsessive about cleanliness. He liked to bathe me often usually about four times a week. I was never allowed to bathe him though. I wasn't clean enough. We did share baths and showers but he would never let me do to him what he obviously felt was his right to do to me. He liked for me to sit all pretty in a huge bath full of bubbles and he would wash me all over. Niko often used the word clean especially when he was having a fit of obsession. It was nice to be pampered, but why wouldn't he let me pamper him? He would often use a whole bottle of expensive bath oil, the towels were gorgeous and fluffy and each one had our own monogram in it. It all seemed so perfect in the beginning, Easy to think this lifestyle was wonderful and just what I wanted. But over time things began to change and not for the better. Niko was getting bored and started to get impatient with many things. Everything was set up for his amusement and never mine. I leant how to behave when he was having a fit, I needed to keep my place so did everything I was told. He began to behave like a madman two to three months later. If I went out to see friends or came home sweaty after some exercise, such as the studio or playing pool he would go crazy and need to bathe me. I had rules you see, I was allowed to dance in the gym, the studio or for competitions but never for fun and certainly not with anyone else only for him. The time when I did dance for fun, I would be punished. At first he would ban me from going out anywhere, I was only allowed to stay in the confines of the grounds on which the house stood, I had to give him everything he wanted and I had to follow his rules regardless of what they were.

He could go away for days at a time when it suits him, but I wasn't allowed anywhere. When he came back from a trip somewhere he became very domineering and I would be allowed to speak ONLY when he permitted and only what he wanted to hear such as:- "I have missed you so much, my life cant go on without you" and many more things in this vein. Like any other red blooded person I became suffocated and I knew that this life wasn't going to get any better and that if I didn't do something about it now I would end up a complete mental case. I had the right to go out if I wished and to make him feel a bit better I wouldn't dress provocatively. Maybe he felt that if I was hanging round anyone I would become dirty and he would then have to bathe me again!

I thought I could sneak out of my window and a few times I managed to get away successfully, when he found out I was locked in my room and the windows were nailed shut so couldn't climb out of them. This was starting to get a bit ridiculous and as a result I was punched in the mouth and it bled quite profusely, that was for disobeying. I wouldn't dare to go out again so I would be under house arrest. Can you imagine what it is like for a person to be deprived of their senses? It completely cuts you off from the world around you.

Over time I noticed that Niko was shouting at many people a lot more than he ever did. He would get upset with people at work and how work was getting him down. Most of the time I had no idea what he was going on about, I just knew he was getting louder and louder. This was the first indication that my life was about to change again! It would become darker before I gathered up the courage to leave. I would no longer feel safe in this house, our paradise that we had built for the two of us. Everyone that I knew was just about to go through hell, my friends, family and me. To this day whenever I have a thought about Niko I get shivers of trepidation and wondering if he was in a good mood or a bad one.

As I am sure you have guessed drugs began to play an important part in our household. Niko had always kept his penchant for cocaine from me until now. I used to smoke pot just for a bit of fun, but if I ever smoked it without him there I would be in trouble. If I had friends in while he wasn't there then I would get a beating. I was not my own person anymore and I had worked myself hard to achieve pride in myself. I was no longer the independent person that moved in with Niko I was a shadow of my former self and things were going to get worse. When I didn't do exactly what he asked I would be shown the error of my ways. Once when I drew his bath for him and the water wasn't hot enough for him he held my head under the water and said it was too cold. I couldn't breathe the chills that went down my spine, and I will never forget that night. I thought at that moment my time had come, I was going to die. I struggled and grabbed Niko's chest attempting to save my own life. I panicked badly and it wasn't until I stayed dead still that he let me go. In an attempt to fight back I watched his every move and learnt his routine and mood swings. I actually thought that if I learnt his moods I would be able to protect myself, I was wrong. I found out that he got a great delight in punishing me, even if I didn't do anything. I began to wear heavy clothing, certainly not my normal clothing. The change of fashion happened because Niko began to start punching me and would often leave large bruises. Due to my bruises I was unable to go to the beach and sunbathe, this made me very sad as it was one of my favourite pastimes.

In he came, through the door slamming it on his way through. The whole house shook. He didn't appear to be in a good mood. I was lazing on the sofa and SLAM! As he stormed through the lounge tearing off his coat he threw his car keys onto the table just missing my ear, the sound of them like a whistle, must have been a hundred miles an hour the rate they were going. He sure had a powerful arm there and now I was seeing the side of him I didn't care much for. He was coming home more and more often in this state. The old feelings of fear were starting to come back. Had I done something to put him in this mood or was it something else.

Niko never really was one to let his feelings show too often and I guess this had been brewing up for a while. Sometimes I wished I was deaf again.

"MAKE ME A DRINK!!!!!" he bellowed. I got up from the sofa and thought

"What the fuck! Who pissed you off today?"

I casually walked to the kitchen to get him his drink a gin and tonic but made sure I slipped plenty of gin in it. He came towards me through the kitchen doorway like a mad man. He grabbed hold of my t-shirt and slung me up against the wall. It kind of took my breath away. His glare was frightening with his eyes turning black, as they usually did when he was not a happy bunny! His stare almost cold as ice and not at all normal. He grabbed the glass from my hand and yelled at me

"I WILL DO IT MYSELF YOU USLESS SHIT!" He screamed at me. I was starting to worry now, I mean, I had seen him in a bad mood but not one this bad! He casually let go of my t-shirt and proceeded to put some tonic over the gin I had already poured for him, he did however, need to top it up as the way he threw me against the wall some of the gin had slopped out of the glass Tears run down my face. While he was putting the tonic in his drink I took the mop from under the sink and cleaned up the mess that had occurred hoping to not anger the beast any more. He looked at me as if I was something he picked up on his shoe. He collected his glass and went to the lounge. As I cleaned the floor I thought to myself

"What the fuck! What have I done to deserve that? Who was this man I had been living with? Why would he just turn like that?" Niko left the kitchen and as he did so I slid down the wall and I sunk to the floor and just sat there, shaking and dumbfounded.

His moods changed from that moment, in fact his whole life changed and our relationship was never the same. To the outside world he was a charming man a generous and benevolent man, but I was now seeing the true Niko, and I didn't like what I was finding out. He was a twisted, cruel and sad man. They do say you cannot keep up a façade in a relationship for too long. Now the beast had reared its ugly head and I have to be honest I was scared.

He began laying out my clothes in the mornings for me. Nice and neat lain on the bed, but the choice of clothing would be Niko's and not mine. If we were going anywhere special he would take me out clothes shopping and choose everything for me. It seemed all he wanted was a trophy on his arm. Things between us started to go from bad to worse and if I didn't obey him and wear what he had picked out for me I would have what clothes I was wearing ripped off and destroyed and then given a beating. Often times I would have to wear long sleeved clothing to cover the purple bruising I would receive at Niko's hand, and it could be pretty embarrassing during the heat of the day. I began to stand out and started getting a bit of a complex about my appearance. After all I was the hottest thing on the island but I was not looking like it anymore. He put a stop to my friends calling too, his reason? He said they were thieving and they didn't belong in Paradisia. Saskia was about the only person allowed entry and that was only if she brought Luis with her. He had been feeding Saskia cocaine for a while now so she was only too pleased to be invited over. After all she knew she would get a hit from Niko and it was quality stuff too. The man, who I absolutely and wholeheartedly trusted with my life, was now turning into a monster. One I didn't like the look of. Had he always been that way? Did I just not see it? Or was he now showing his true colours? He was a pig!!!! If I did not respond in the way he wanted me to I would get kicked all around the kitchen. In the end I became immune to the pain. I felt numb most of the time. He would pull my hair, run me down in the car, pinch me and now he was resorting to actually beating me black and blue. Why? I repeatedly asked myself. What have I done to deserve this treatment? All I had ever done was idolised and adore Niko. I felt like an animal kept in a cage in fear of its life. After beating me; sometimes to within inches of death, he would want to make love to me.

"I am sorry Christian!" he would always say, whilst I was still on my knees giving him what he wanted and enjoyed most.

One night whilst we were settling down for bed we watched a gay porn film. Niko loved these films; he would watch them and then try what he had seen out on me. The videos we particularly watched were into bondage and Niko was charged up on Viagra at the time. Niko started to fantasise and while he was watching what was happening he began his tirade of physical abuse on me. At first he began with candle wax and whips, which I submitted to. I can't believe I am going to say this but I could handle the wax and whips just fine. He came to the point where he wanted me to prove my love for him. He told me he was going to do something to me and I was to feel nothing but him while he was doing it. I was not to complain or make a noise while it happened. I was frightened, I couldn't imagine the pain he planned to inflict on me while I lay on the bed waiting with my eyes closed and quite frankly, praying for my life. I can not tell you what fear came over me. I cannot believe the horrors I had endured from someone who purportedly loved me. He got rather sexually excited on hurting me both in the physical and the psychological sense. While I was waiting for the next torture to occur he started touching me all over whilst I lay on the bed. It felt good, I became excited and erect. He held me, kissed me and I felt great. I became more relaxed and not so scared thinking the torture was over. He was shouting and the music was very loud and I couldn't hear him properly. I could "hear" and feel the vibrations. He told me to look at him while he touched me and I was to look into his eyes. I could only see the whites of his eyes since the room was dark and the light only shone on his face. It was a horrific sight and I became very scared. It was as if one of my nightmares was coming true. I saw his eyes soften with lust and I think a bit of hidden evil too. He started laughing out loud and lit a cigarette. I often thought I would love to know what was going on in his head. He leant over and put his hand across my mouth tight and stared into my eyes.

"Do you love me Christian?" He asked through his teeth.

"How much do you love me?" he asked as he pulled back the duvet from me. I did not know how to take his mood. I was a little shaken to say the least but he laid his hand across my tummy while he looked me up and down. All went quiet and he took one look at me but all I could see were his black eyes staring at me full of madness, little did I know what was about to happen.

"I SAID!!!!!! HOW MUCH DO YOU LOVE ME!?" and he placed his hand a little further down.

"THIS MUCH??" I screamed as he stabbed his lit cigarette on my manhood. I instantly broke into tears the pain excruciating. I felt as if I was on fire. All he could do was laugh at me; he didn't show an ounce of remorse. He must have held the cigarette in place for at least ten seconds, it seemed a lifetime.

The tears just fell in rivulets down my face. The next split second I was being flung onto my front with such force. This was NOT pleasurable in any way. It took the pain of my burn away but it was substituted with a new pain, one I would remember for along time. After he had taken what pleasure he could, he threw me off the bed and yelled at me. I suppose this was one of the few times during the latter part of our relationship, if you could call it that, that I actually pleased him, but at what cost to me? With the Viagra he could go for hours, thankfully this last time lasted just an hour. I cried all the way through it, every minute. He should have been locked away in some institution for the mentally deranged. I am sure he would have killed me eventually searching for that ultimate sexual gratification. I realised after that event that Niko had to be completely morally bankrupt and with no conscience whatsoever.

"Go shower now you slut! Clean yourself up!!!" I felt dirty. Used an abused my heart was breaking. I had given this man everything I had to give and this is how he treats me. I went to the bathroom, locked the door and leant against the wall. The tears were coming thick and fast and as I began to cry uncontrollably I slid down the wall into the foetal position on the floor. I cried until I could cry no more, begging and pleading for someone to help me. Nobody came.

One time he stabbed me too. I had been out on the town one afternoon; I was dressed all in white with shorts t-shirt socks and trainers. I had stopped at a couple of bars to have a few drinks and a couple of games of pool with my friends. I was very well known in the village as everyone knew who Niko was. I had many friends, both gay and straight. You might say I was a stranger to no one. I had gone to about four bars before I started to feel the effects of ouzo. I suppose in general I am a happy drunk and was a little daring. This particular night I was dancing with my shirt off, I had a pretty good body so why shouldn't I? With the bravery that the ouzo gave me I jumped onto a raised platform and began to dance. The previous bar I was in had a patron who was a friend of Niko's. This guy gave Niko a call and told him what I was doing. In almost a split second I turned round and faced the door and there propping up the wall was Niko and he didn't look very happy. He simply said "HOME!" and he left. There was nothing left that he could do to me, apart from kill me, and I didn't want to live very much at this point anyway. I finished my drink and put my shirt back on. I made my way to another bar and drank a little more ouzo and had some fun. I had to make sure I was totally drunk when I came face to face with Niko. I couldn't have done it any other way. When I reached the back door to the house I began praying before I entered. The lights came on whilst I was standing there, I knew he was home and I was going to get severely beaten again! I didn't need to knock as the door was already open. I passed into the kitchen, Niko lunged at me like a lunatic, shouting, raving and throwing things. He was shouting things like "You like people to look at you huh!? You like to take your clothes off for them huh!?" He was pulling my hair, long at the time, and pulled my head hard backwards and looked into my eyes and at my lips. He did not want me to miss a word he said. It was pretty brightly lit at this time so I was able to read his lips pretty well. I looked at him wondering what I ever saw in this man. He had decided that I was not fit enough or clean enough for him especially in the white clothes he had bought me. He ripped off my shirt and shorts and pulled my hair out in handfuls. He called me all the names he could think of in Greek, I was a whore and several other things he threw at me.

I had not seen anything in his hand when he came in but it was there. I was already in pain from the many slaps and pushes and ripping out my hair. I didn't really know if it was his intention but he ripped my shorts off so fast, I felt an intense pain on my left side between my ribs. I felt all warm then everything went black, I must have passed out. After coming to I felt a lot of pain and I had been wrapped up and taken to my bedroom. Niko was nowhere to be seen. The family doctor was there talking to someone. I thought it might be Niko but it wasn't. The doctor gave me dirty looks as if I was an idiot. Well, I suppose I was really after having been stabbed and beaten up by the man who supposedly loved me. I expect he wondered why I put up with it. After that event I spent a lot of time sleeping, just to get my body back to some semblance of order.

One particular day I had held my morning class teaching traditional Greek dance in the studio and then spent the afternoon in town, you know, doing what you do, dancing, shopping and wishing and shopping some more. I made my way home. On the way I had given previous events at Paradisia a whole lot of thought. Did I really understand the man? Was I now witnessing a total change in personality or was this the REAL Niko? I hoped it wasn't the latter. I arrived at the back entrance to Paradisia and went through the back door into the kitchen where I stumbled over Saskia as I put my foot through the door. She was crumpled up in a heap and clutching at her mouth; I looked up and saw Niko standing over her. It was obvious that she had just been on the receiving end of Niko's new found temper. Every bone in my body shook, every beat of my heart getting closer and closer together, I clutched my chest and breathed a heavy sigh. I screamed at Niko "NOT HER!!!!!!!!" I looked down as he slapped me straight across the face, my eyes falling on Saskia almost fighting for life, quickly followed by the rest of me quivering as I fell from Niko's reeling blow. We laid there in this heap for what seemed like hours, it was only for a short time, just enough for Niko to maybe think we were dead and leave us alone. He left the kitchen slamming doors and stomping up the marble staircase. I had to protect Saskia for Luis' sake. I slowly moved my position and got off Saskia as quickly as I could, each move more painful than the last I must have broken a rib! I looked down at Saskia, her mouth swollen and cut where she had been on the end of Niko's fist. I ran some clean water onto a cloth and slowly and gingerly dabbed the sore area on her mouth, trying to clean some of the blood away. As I dabbed she flinched, in obvious agony for what she has just been subjected to. She lifted herself slowly from the floor as the coolness of the cloth had started to revive her. As I held her in my arms to try and convince her that it would never happen again she said

"I am SO sorry Christian!"

"Saskia, don't worry this IS going to stop I promise you" I replied sternly not having a clue how I was going to carry out what I had just promised her. I held her tight to my chest and rocked her just a little to reassure her.

"I am going to MAKE him stop!!" I muttered to myself through gritted teeth. I had to think now how I was going to accomplish this and went to bed and tossed and turned all night. I was going to be submissive for a while to work things out. I took in everything that was happening and walked around Paradisia like a zombie. I was just going to do what I was told and bide my time. This behaviour needed to stop now before he killed someone!!

He had now done the same to Saskia that he was doing with me and I couldn't let it happen to another human being, let alone Saskia. We may have had our problems but at the end of the day she was "family" and you looked after your own.

CHAPTER 11

THE FATHER

I was glad when Thursday came round. I knew Niko would be tied up in meetings all day. I felt free and able to breathe and just be glad to be alive. The situation at Paradisia was getting worse by the day. This particular day I had gone into town to shop for some new denims. I already had a closet full of them but I felt I was in need of a little retail therapy. That morning as he left for "the office" he threw a wad of money at me and told me to go away and leave him to do "family business". It felt great just walking around the town free as a bird, no yelling going on, no flinching in case I got hit. I promised myself that I was not going to let any of that bother me today I was out and almost skipping down the street, carriers in hand wafting in the breeze. I smelled a gorgeous smell in the air wafting down the street filling my nostrils with all sorts of good smells. Mmmmmmmm I had to have something to eat. I went into the little Greek Cafe where the delicious mouth watering smells came from. I sat down at the first table I could find that had been cleaned away, it was a busy day and the café had quite a few patrons. A waiter soon came over to me. Smiling as they had been taught to do, always to please the customer, and then when they go out the back you just know they are going to gossip or gob in your food. I got the feeling that the waiter knew me from somewhere. I thought for a moment and he gave me some recognition that he knew who I was. Then it came to me he had been in Adonis. I hadn't really taken much notice of him then as my eyes were permanently fixed on Niko. But he looked kind of interesting. Anyway, I digress, I saw a few of my friends from the dance class and they were quite surprised to see me. I hadn't been out much of late as I had to cover up quite a bit and I felt as if all eyes would be on me. I always wore my trademark sunglasses, so not many people were any the wiser and we just passed pleasantries. After we all greeted and shook hands I ordered from the nice waiter a huge double cheeseburger with fries, salad and a glass of coke. I was tucking into my lunch and I just took a couple of glances coming my way. Being able to lip read put me in a good position I was able to work out what most people were talking about.

One conversation grabbed me. They were the glances I was getting and I worked out they were talking about me; they looked at me then looked away and laughed and then looked again. It was all pretty juvenile really but this particular conversation had me riveted to the spot. I knew them a little through Saskia and it was her they were talking about also.

"Saskia is such a slag! She's got that kid and can't even take care of it properly" They muttered. I was amazed at what was being said! Did I read that right?

"The father is so rich that's why she's like that stupid!" The dark haired girl added.

"Oh yeah! Who feeds her drugs" The blonde girl replied. "WHAT!" I heard screaming in my head. How come they knew Luis' father and I didn't! I had a nasty feeling in the pit of my stomach, it churned away like it was blending cheese. I really needed to get to Saskia and ask her first hand. I was not going to take gossip for real. After all the whole country was full of gossip mongers and I wasn't going to be one of them. I finished eating my meal, drank my coke, stood up with a bit of force, and strode over to the table these girls were sitting at. I put my hands on their table really softly waited for a second or two and BANNNGG I hit that table so hard it seemed to vibrate all around the café. The girls jumped and probably shit themselves, the whole place looking at me I said in a very loud voice so that I could be understood

"I would shut your mouths if I was you!!! DO YOU UNDERSTAND ME!!!!!?"

Then I casually walked out, I needed to see Saskia as soon as I could praying all the while that my fears were wrong.

Saskia was due home about 2pm. Her mother was having Luis for the afternoon. I was out in the back garden when she arrived. She kicked off her shoes in the hallway and came out to me smiling.

"Hi Christian! What's happening?" She asked just as she did every time we met.

"I'm cool" I replied smiling and nodding my head as I lit up a joint. We often smoked green together. I gave up the powder many months ago but Saskia was up for most things.

"Sask I have a lot going on in my head at the moment while I was in the café I saw two girls talking together about you!" I said looking at her and passing the smoke. She took it and toked quite hard on the spliff.

"Christian! You do surprise me listening to gossip from idiots. Who was talking about me anyway?" She questioned.

"Doesn't matter who it was does it? Who is Luis' father Saskia?" I pushed at her, she was completely shocked her mouth gaping open and fear in her eyes. "What!?" she said with surprise on her face. She looked as if she was a rabbit caught in the headlamps.

"WHO THE FUCK IS IT? WHO IS LUIS' FATHER? TELL ME NOW!!!!" I screamed that one in her face like a roaring lion.

Saskia looked at the floor. She was crying. "Christian I am SO Sorry!" She sobbed.

"Fucking hell Saskia!!! Just tell me NOW!" I pleaded with her.

"NIKO! Niko is Luis' father" She said shaking from her head to her toes.

"I can't remember Christian; I promise you I was high on drugs! I am so sorry" she said quivering before me rivers of tears running down her face. I was absolutely mortified. My best friend had slept with my lover and my so called best friend was telling me that Luis was the outcome!

"Jesus Christ Saskia! How long has this been going on?" I asked her needing to know the whole truth this time. I was sick of being lied to, so now it STOPS! My thought processes started and all sorts of events and feelings were rushing through my head like a set of white water rapids! *Oh MY! I had been at Luis' birth, I was the first man to hold him, and they even thought I was his dad. No wonder Saskia was always on top and taking care of things and visited and stayed whenever she liked.*

"Niko swore me to silence Christian, you have to believe me he would have killed me if I had let on to anyone least of all tell YOU!" She confessed through her tear and mascara stained face

"YOU FUCKING SLAG, YOU BITCH, WHORE!!!!!!!! HOW COULD YOU SASKIA?" I screamed obscenities at her for all I was worth. I was discovering feelings I never knew I had. Such anger where did it come from? I put my hands on her shoulders and just kept shouting at her. I was very hurt inside and angry but I felt for her nonetheless. I now knew who Niko truly was and how he could be. I had to get out of this mad house!

The house stood in all its glory, but at the same time looked a sad house. I stood outside on the gravel driveway, the sun shining and a cool breeze blowing. I thought about the fun times we had when we began our relationship but then those thoughts became over shadowed by Niko's latest ramblings and violence toward Saskia and me. I became unimpressed with the house, for all its lavishness and beauty it became a place I could not be happy and cosy as I had felt I would be. Maybe that was just a dream! But then who knows what is round the next corner you come to in life. I should have listened to Mama when she forbade me to go to Niko. I had made my bed and now I had to lie in it and I certainly wasn't going back to Mama's house if I left Paradisia.

I lay restless in bed that last night. Niko slept heavily and I could hear his snoring and spluttering. The moon was shining through the wooden shutters on the windows, the sound of the night birds singing in the trees made for an odd night. The clouds drifting quite quickly due to the breeze continuing from earlier on in the day but with the sun going down it became quite chilly with that wind blowing. My bed became a disaster zone with each and every turn raking up the sheet and coming together underneath me. I got out of bed and re made the bed. I went to the fridge to get a glass of milk to try and induce some sleep. Mama always swore by it for a restless night, warm milk mmmmmm I drifted back to those times when I was happy with Mama and our life so simple together. I wandered back to bed to take my place of rest for the night. As I lay my head on the pillow flashes started and all the recent events that Paradisia had witnessed came back and questions developed quickly racing one after the other almost blowing my mind. *He took Saskia! I mean he fucked her and got her pregnant with Luis. He treated ME like a dog! He took and took and took from whomever he came into contact with and these people went on to be beholden to him, to submit to his every demand! WOW that was some achievement… Having people literally eating out of your hand, no wonder he threw his weight around.*

People from the villages, the top families, the bars and clubs, none of them liked Niko; they lived in fear of him, afraid of what he would do at any moment. He might have bought me a fast flash car with the number plate "boy 1". He may have bought me my own dance studio but I had paid heavily with my innocence. I had wheels to get around and a regular income coming in and believe me I would need that to support the three of us, Saskia, Luis and myself. I was not going to turn my back on them. Luis and I were very close now and Niko was not going to take that away ever!

He went to work at 9 am, suited and booted as usual, briefcase and smelling as good as he ever did. I lay in bed while he laid out my clothes for the day. I pretended to be asleep, trying so hard to keep my eyeballs still as you do when one is in pretence mode. I am unsure whether he could sense I was pretending or not but he kissed me on the forehead.

"See you tonight around six Christian!" he grabbed his briefcase and left. I waited until I heard the sound of his car disappear as far as I could. I got up out of the bed and made the decision to go right that second. My heart began to pump making my chest hurt, I knew that if I was ever going to do it the time was now! I quickly gathered a few belongings together in a rucksack which I had kept in the bottom of my wardrobe. I didn't pay much attention to tidiness I just had to get out. I hurriedly pulled on my jeans and a t-shirt, I left the clothes he had put out for me right where he left them. I grabbed whatever I could lay my hands on as I made straight for the front door. I was shit scared I don't mind telling you, but I was quite excited too. I wasn't going to be THAT mans punch bag or doormat anymore. I grabbed all the loose money lying around, it amounted quite a bit but I didn't have the time to count it. I found his cigarettes in a box on the table by the sofa and took the whole thing! Yes the whole thing! I would be able to smoke all the cigarettes in it and maybe sell it when I was finding things a bit tough. If I ever did find things bad I still had my dance studio I could fall back on to earn a fair bit to keep us all happy together. In the bottom drawer of his desk there was a huge bag of green, so that came with me as well, at least I could find a bit of peace once in a while. I did not make the bed or do the washing up of the breakfast things. BOLLOCKS!!!!! I just didn't care any more. I should have smashed up the whole house then doused it in petrol and set light to it, oh! Believe me! The thought had crossed my mind but I put it out of my mind. No I would think of a better plan for him! I think losing me was going to be more than enough damage to his master! Did I leave a note for him? You bet your life I did! Should I wait here for him to come home and then tell him it was over? OH MY GOD!!!! I had to go right now this minute, if I didn't I would never go. I reached the front door went outside a breath of clean fresh air hitting my nostrils; I turned around and locked the door, held the keys in my hand for a few seconds and then CLANG! The keys had gone through the letter box and hit the marble floor below.

Oh well! I had done it now, I stood back from the house took one more long look, breathed a heavy sigh thought to myself. *How could such dreams be so badly shattered in such a short time?* I adored that man and would have done anything for him, but he had finally broken my spirit and my heart. It was a beautiful house with breathtaking surrounds, I would miss it but that was it I was leaving it all behind to move onto pastures new. Something told me I would be here again though. I didn't know when or why but I would be back this was not going to be my last time at Paradisia.

As I stood there one hand on the door handle of the car and looking at Paradisia it brought to mind a video I had seen on the internet. It was a song Shirley Bassey sang called "This is My Life" The words of the song captured my feelings at that moment and from then on whenever I felt down I would sing this song to myself and as the song goes "I don't give a damn!" It set the scene for the rest of my life, Niko had done his worst to me and I was NOT going to let him get me down and ruin my life. It was now in my hands and I had every intention of being a success in whatever I chose to do.

CHAPTER 12

GIO

I had known Gio all of my life really. He was also born in Corfu in the same town I was. He was a little older than me by 3 years. I used to see him at school and on the beach with his family at weekends. He would sometimes be dating a girl for a while but nothing ever too serious ever became of those. We became very strong friends when I was about 17 and he would be 20. He worked in the nearby bar as a bar man and he worked most evenings and weekends... He was olive skinned and about 6 foot tall with an athletic build. His hair was jet black with a tint of red in it and fell shoulder length, His eyes were brown and he had a beauty spot on his left cheek by his mouth. His eyelashes were very long and his nails so clean and perfect – oh and he had wonderful white teeth too gleaming like tombstones. He was a stunning looking guy with a body to die for.

Gio knew Niko and he knew Saskia too. He had seen Saskia growing up and had accepted her as part of my company. Gio was just "sex on legs" to Saskia, she fancied him something rotten but the feelings were not reciprocated. He was more of a girl than she was at times. When Luis came along he often babysat for him when Saskia wanted to go out and get off her face. He was reliable and trustworthy, and these were only two of his special qualities. Niko didn't like Gio being at our house, mainly I think because he was jealous he knew there was chemistry between us and he didn't like it. Gio wasn't really worried about Niko even though he was abusive and rude, this went straight over Gio's head, he just carried on in his polite way even when Niko was rude to him and kicked him out.

I had been calling him on and off for the last few days telling him I had to leave Paradisia as soon as I could and I may need a place to stay for a while. He told me I was more than welcome to stay with him for as long as I wished. I just could not go back to Mama.

It was directly after I left Paradisia that I went to Gio. I parked my car, grabbed my rucksack slung it over my shoulder and knocked on the door.

"Christian! Oh my! Are you ok?" He asked as he opened the door and threw his arms round me and held me close. He knew what I had been through and I knew I could trust him. He took my hand and led me into the lounge dropping my rucksack in the hall. I slumped on the sofa breathing a HEAVY sigh of relief. At last! I could breathe and be safe. While Gio went to make tea I just rolled out everything that had happened

"Gio! I can't take it anymore. I just can't!" and I burst into tears. Sometimes crying uncontrollably, after all I had trusted Niko with my life and all I got was abuse both mentally and physically.

"It's ok Christian! You are safe here and I wont let him come anywhere near you and I will always be here for you. I will not let you down" He said reassuringly. I snuggled into him and felt warm and cosy. I stayed there for ages Gio stroking my hair and my face to make me feel safe. He rolled a rather large joint and we sat and chilled out and Gio just sat and listened; no judgment came from his lips.

"Stay with me in my bed tonight Christian" He asked "Its ok, we will be ok"

"I can take the sofa Gio is no problem" I said to him

"Nah! Its ok Chris share my bed, its more comfortable and you will sleep better and right now sleep is what you need" That night we spent together doped out of our heads holding each other close. I had not felt so cared for in a long time. I thought I had that with Niko but how wrong could I have been?

I woke at 6am; I looked over to Gio and watched him sleep for a while. He was sleeping soundly and I just sat and looked at how beautiful he was. I stared at him for a while and thoughts of Niko came into my head, he too had that look once upon a time. I quietly raised myself from the bed and headed for the shower. I took a look in the mirror *OH MY GOD!!!!!!* What a nightmare to look at. I showered and shaved and made myself feel at least half decent. I put on my jeans and sprayed myself with some of Gio's body spray. Walking to the kitchen to make a cup of tea I still had all the thoughts going around in circles in my head. I made a cup of tea and sat on the sofa in the lounge. I guess I must have fallen asleep as I awoke to Gio singing at the top of his voice whilst cooking up breakfast. Boy! He was cheerful in the mornings; always smiling and he was a good cook too so I would be sure of something good for breakfast. I used to be like that once. How could I have let it get so disastrously wrong?

Soon it would be common knowledge that I was staying at Gio's but there was no way I could go back to Mama's house. At least I still had my studio, Niko may have bought it but everything was in my name so I would carry on running it. It worked well staying with Gio. I worked during the days and he mainly worked at night so we both had our own space but we were there for each other. We did however, continue to share the bedroom and that was nice too. Saskia would visit in the evening with Luis and she would stay until I had to say to her

"That boy should be in his bed Sask!" I would say reminding her that she had responsibilities, and off she would go struggling to be a mother but very sad because of the effect the amount of cocaine she had partaken of had destroyed her.

On the first Friday night of being single I decided to go into town and shoot some pool with my friends. The place was buzzing. We were in the bar chatting and laughing and catching up on what had been happening, then, all of a sudden it felt like the sky had just caved in on me. I lifted my head and there he was!!!!! I saw him at the bar downing a few neat brandies. He had seen me.

Everywhere I seemed to go Niko would be there. I had seen him in bars and cafes here and there. I had several confrontations with him when he was trying to meet me and I refused. One of the times we confronted each other I had had enough and punched him in the face. He was stunned but he never got the chance to hit me back as when I threw the punch we were both restrained in the bar and pulled apart. I got a good punch and it left a bruise on his face. I hate to say it but I did feel pretty good about doing that. He treated me very badly and now he was going to get some of his own medicine. Whether it be in a café to eat or in a bar shooting some pool .He never approached me like he once did before, I think he knew I would fight back now. He would just stare and occasionally send over a drink which I always refused. He was still staying in Paradisia. He knew I was staying at Gio's place and I knew he was just choosing his time to deal with Gio. I knew what he was capable of. He didn't go to the dance studio anymore as if he did show up I would go and get cover and simply leave. He didn't impose on my work; he for similar reasons respected the work place. For that I was grateful as I could then have semblance of order in my life while I came to terms with the break up. But this one night he couldn't help himself. He just had to say something.

"YOU COMING HOME CHRISTIAN!!!" he shouted embarrassing me in front of my friends. I took one look at him and placed the pool cue on the table turned to Gio and said

"I am going home are you coming Gio. I really can't face what he has to dish out tonight" My eyes pleading that he would heed my wish. We grabbed our keys and left hand in hand. I really didn't want to go through a fight in my local pool hall. That wasn't very dignified. Gio and I got in the Audi and sped off home. When we arrived we went into the kitchen and poured ourselves a glass of red wine then took them into the lounge and sat peacefully together listening to some of our favourite music. The evening had the potential to be a violent one but I knew I was safe with Gio. We spent many a quiet hour together just listening to music and talking. We had so much in common. He was not only a gentleman he was also a gentle man a rare commodity in my life.

Some weekends we would both talk together and we would chill all day and all night. We would lie on the beach for a couple of hours and then swim together. Although we both had beautiful complexions and the perfect olive skin – nothing looked better than looking all tanned up and bronzed! Anyway all the time we would smoke joints and get mellow. We would laze around the house listening to all sorts of music both feeling high as kites! I would dance sometimes and he would watch me. He always got an openly shown erection watching me dance; his Lycra showed it all leaving nothing to the imagination. We would dance together too sometimes holding each other close and feel each other, I mean lets face it Lycra and Denim together WOW! On occasions I would just pounce on him, stick my tongue down his throat and kept going, then I would suck hard on his tongue and it drove him wild! He was definitely hot and our kissing sessions happened often but no more than just that. Gio was the greatest with Luis and you could see just how much Luis adored Gio. They were beginning to form a bond together; Saskia had been up and down with her life so on the times that she wasn't being a fit and able mother and when I had to work Gio would look after Luis. Sometimes Luis would be more pleased to see Gio than his own mother. I could not fully commit to Gio though. I guess others would have called him *"my bitch!"* He was happy to be there.

Luis was staying with us more or less full time now because Saskia was disappearing more and more. She only cared for taking coke and having a good time. She was a mess. Gio and I both knew we had to take over with Luis. Gio often told her to pull herself together before she totally lost Luis. But it was not enough. She flirted with Gio and it disgusted him.

CHAPTER 13

FAMILY BUSINESS

I had learnt, through watching Niko, and checking the bank accounts, that all the money being made was not just obtained from making olive oil and selling it. Niko's great-grandfather had started the olive oil business. He used the land he owned to plant olive trees everywhere he could and it just grew from there. He was well regarded as an olive oil expert who personally tested and selected the precise blend of oils sold. He was a leader in the export market for olive oil. Literally hundreds of tons of oil made in Corfu were sent on the transatlantic journey to the United States in the 1800s, where it was eagerly purchased by Italian-American immigrants, hungry for a taste of home. The olive trees are tended with loving care year round and they have an abundance of flowers allowing the olives to reach their optimal size and maturity just before they are harvested. In was drummed into each of the members of their family the eight step process to gain a successful crop and therefore having the lifestyle they were able to enjoy. It all became a part of life and much the same as we live our lives – harvesting, crushing, selecting, tasting, analysing, refining, blending, and packing. Each one of these steps can be attributed to some process in our lives. In Greece olives were said to have been created by the Goddess Athena and were so esteemed that only "virgins" and "chaste men" could tend the groves for the purity. Olives were a rare and precious commodity to lovers of fine foods and still are today for the discerning palate. Among the first written records olive oil were inventory logs carried by ancient trading ships which brought olive oil along the many routes through the Mediterranean. They were introduced to Greece as a luxurious import; olive oil was not only prized as a food but also as a beauty treatment and lightly scented fuel for lamps. So it was in great demand and therefore was a very lucrative business which was handed down as far back as I can remember from father to son, which is how it fell into Nikos hands and therefore providing the lifestyle he had and left him free to be the person he was and not a very nice one at that! It had been many years but Niko still owned the land bequeathed to him He never worked on the land, you have got to be kidding me! He had plenty of workers to do that for him and he sat back and reaped in the profits. He imported from all around the world and I am sure there was not just olive oil! Men would call at the house often and I would be told to "go practice your dance hunny!" by Niko. I would see them come in; sometimes just one man other times two or three. They would kiss Niko on the hand and then the office door would shut. They would never be in there for longer than an hour but when the door opened brandies would have been drunk and smiles would abound. I often would ask Niko what had been going on after he had received his visitors

"Family business Christian! Nothing for you to worry about!" was all he would say and just dismiss me like a child. I knew there was something going on as Niko would always be seen emptying a bag or case full of money into the safe. What did he really think I was? A fool!? That was something that Niko really didn't appreciate was my mind. I was not stupid and I had a pretty good idea what was going on. One day I would find out. I would keep my cool and just take whatever he dished out. My time would come in the not too distant future, I was sure of that. I knew it was more than money from the olive oil business he was reaping. I assumed he was into drugs given how he had been with Saskia and how drugged up she always seemed to be. After a few weeks I found out it was not just drug money he was taking but protection money from the small businesses around , also there was evidence I saw that he was a pimp too for the local whores. Niko had his hands in it all. He had been collecting rent from the local shop owners and bars for protection. This turned my stomach. Some of these people had inherited their business from their families and had worked all their lives to earn a decent living. Even though I wasn't happy about it I had some research on the quiet and found that it was Niko who was controlling the amount of money people paid for the protection racket as the other cartels around would be charging a lot more and would be a lot more violent if they didn't get their dues. THAT is why everyone was almost licking his boots! Why everyone bowed and scraped to Niko because he was the cheaper and it seemed at the time softer option. He owned a lot of people in the cage fighting business and the whores he ran too. Both of them each a dirty business to work in and they were being managed by him. He had no feelings for people in matters of business. I found out he got involved with cage fighting when he was a young man. He had watched a few fights and saw how easy it was to make money in the line of business. He owned property and usually won gambling. People used to give him all sorts when they were in such fear of him.

Drugs were always on hand, but I thought he was a bit of an idiot to use the stuff he was selling. It was a bit like giving an alcoholic a pub to run, not a good idea! Imagine that after a while! I remember Niko introducing me to cocaine. The first time we took it together we had such a beautiful evening of closeness and making love. I did not keep on taking it though as I did not like the feel of coming down off it and it made my nose sore too. I was just going to stick to my ganja! Niko snorted regularly, probably about £50 up his nose every hour. He carried it off well though; you couldn't really tell he was under the influence of it much. He had been doing it a while so I guess he just got used to it and knew how to deal with it. He always was clean and well turned out and had great pride in his appearance, although how he managed that under the influence of cocaine all the time I will NEVER know! Some of the whores he pimped worked in the high street. I have to say though that he did treat them reasonably well they used to have regular health checks to make sure they didn't pass anything on that was unhealthy or worse still life threatening. Trade was always busy during the summer months and as a result Niko was rolling in cash. All of his businesses were backed up by drug money. Everyone wanted money for their drugs and all the time it was Nikos profit going into his coffers.

Other people used to come to the house too. Ordinary people, if that's not being too rude. Still the door to the den would be shut whilst he entertained them in whatever capacity they needed his help and advice. This was the time when I knew that EVERYONE respected and looked to Niko to sort their problems out. In return he "owned" them. This was how he became so powerful in our village and the ones nearby too. He was a very generous man, especially towards me, I was very thankful for the life he had introduced me too, but somehow it didn't seem right to accept any more after I had found out how he obtained his money. He gave heavy donations to the Church and the local hospice. He would always keep an eye out for any small business that was going under, then offer to bail the proprietor out and then he would own them. He always took in vulnerable cases. He was a very money orientated kind of guy; it seemed as if he had nothing else going on in his life that made him happy, until I came along.

I once used tactics to get a problem I had swiftly sorted out. I told Niko that Toni was giving Mama such a hard time, he was pushing her about and a couple of times I had noticed a few bruises that she tried to hide from me and he would still fail to give Mama any money to live on. He was ill treating her to the point that it made her days very depressing and she started to slide into ill health. Niko listened with intent and said that he would sort it out for me. His words were

"Consider it sorted baby!" a chilling look on his face. Toni was never to be seen again.

CHAPTER 14

NIKO'S DEATH

Saskia went to visit Niko on a regular basis, mainly to get her fixes. She often told me how different he was with Luis. He took him out and bought him whatever he desired, they would go swimming together, Niko would read Luis stories and they just generally spent most of their time together. These actions by Niko feared me even more. I couldn't let Niko get close to Luis and allow him to warp Luis' mind to his way of life. There was no way I was going to allow Niko to hurt Luis. I told Saskia – in fact I demanded she didn't take Luis to visit Niko anymore. She didn't really want Luis in Niko's life but by doing so she got everything she wanted. When she told Niko what I had said he demanded that BOTH Saskia and I were to go to Paradisia for dinner to discuss Luis and his welfare. He said to arrive at 7pm and we could have some drinks before dinner. *Bring it on*!

I thought. I wasn't scared of him any longer and I wasn't going to let him get his evil claws in Luis.

Saskia got ready with me at Gio's house. She wore a beautiful long chocolate brown dress with matching shoes. She had her hair done and made up her face. I have to be honest she really did look nice. If only she made that much of an effort all the time. My attire consisted of as normal white denims with a silk white shirt. I shaved up a mean goatee and tied my hair back. You would've thought to look at us we were going clubbing not to Niko's for dinner, but an invite from Niko meant you had to pull all stops out and look your best. We learnt to dress for the occasion.

I started up the Audi and off we went; it wasn't far from Gio's really just around the corner. The thoughts came flooding back of the last time I was at Paradisia and I had to shake myself out of it and bring myself back to the reason I was going to Paradisia again, this was for Luis. The one thing in my life I wasn't going to allow Niko to destroy. My music playing at full volume almost, the windows down and the wind in our hair I said to Saskia

"Let's go for a spin before we go to that bastard's house eh Sask!" and pulled out a couple of huge joints from my shirt pocket. I passed one to Saskia and we sparked them both up. She looked at me every now and then, feeling the tenseness I was feeling.

"Sask! Don't worry hun! I won't let him come near you ok, I promise you!" I told her this loud and I felt brave for the words I had spoken. We parked up the car and puffed away on our joints.

"You smell soooooo good Sask!" I said trying a Yankee accent. She smiled

"You are mad Christian but look – about everything, I am really sorry you know, but I am glad I have you in my life still" she looked at me searchingly

"No matter what Saskia, I will always fend for you and look after Luis I love you both!" I kissed her on the forehead. We sat for about 5 minutes smoking away and trying to get our heads in the right frame of mind for what was to come.

"OK Sask! Let's go face the bastard!" I said grasping her hand in reassurance.

She chilled a little after that and gave me a look which told me everything would be fine. I glanced at her as if to say would it!?

We parked up outside Paradisia sat there for a few minutes. I held her hand; every fibre of my being was absorbed in contemplation of our meeting with Niko.

"Ready?" I asked her clenching my hand on hers. We were in this together now and we knew we had a lot to deal with. Just as we looked for the handle to leave the car BANG! There he was!

"Hello – both of you!" He said with THAT grin on his face that tried to tell us we were going to be persuaded to do something we didn't want to do. He thought he was all that dressed in his blue Armani suit. His scent wafted all around.

"Welcome, welcome come on in" he said with a look which reminded me of a saying "Come on in" said the spider to the fly as soon as the door was shut she ate the fly! This I held onto I didn't trust him at all.

We went into the house, boy! It felt so strange being back here. I looked all around and nothing had changed. Still the same décor, still the same pretence, and worst of all STILL the same old Niko. The dining table was all prepared stretched out before us in the dining room adorned with all manner of decoration. Our drinks in our places, who was he to assume that I wanted what he was providing, not even a "What would you like to drink" had been uttered. Saskia was given a vodka and coke and in my place sat a Jack Daniels. As usual Niko didn't cook and he gave the servants the night off, so we were fed Pizza from the take away. We had Pizza, garlic bread, coleslaw, chips and salads. He was drinking brandy like it was going out of fashion. I stayed silently mostly and let Niko and Saskia converse about what they wanted for Luis. He was rather drunk and Saskia was getting slightly merry on the vodka. Then true to form he pulled out a bag of cocaine.

"Oh! You don't mind do you? – I know you may want some Saskia" he said pushing the bag towards her. He knew every move he was making; I was not falling for his charm. He pulled out his little mirror which he kept in his inside pocket and rolled up a note. He didn't have a care in the world; he was sitting in his castle drinking his fine brandy and snorting his sad drugs. He looked pathetic and ugly and old too! He would often say "My son this" "My son that!" "My heir this" and "My heir that!" I had heard it a thousand times over and over again during those few hours we were there, and it was killing me inside. Saskia was well gone by now, having drunk as much as she could get down her neck and snorted the coke that was so freely given by Niko! Damn! What a let down she was. I had told her I would stick by her but now I was starting to feel betrayed by her. So much for my promises! She looked a state not like the beautiful young woman she had started out as that evening. I took a step back and sat watching them both for a while. Many thoughts came into my head, but the one which had the most impact was

"How the hell have I not seen that before!!!!!!" They both suited each other and at that moment I could see that neither of them was going to change. I could see how easily they had come together and produced Luis. A poor innocent child brought into a drug ridden, bullying, power controlled life! I was even more determined now to not let Niko have anything to do with Luis. I couldn't stop Saskia from seeing and mixing with Niko, but I sure as hell wasn't going to allow Luis to be ruined but such a society. They both made me sick! I sipped on my JD, I think I only had two all night; smoked a little green while they did their stuff. I hated Pizza too and Niko knew that. Just another dig in the ribs, when was he going to stop! He knew there was no way I was going back to him. Little things like the Pizza business brought it home to me just how much he wanted to control my life. I had wised up and things were going to change now. He always treated me as the less important one, simply because I wouldn't pander to his wishes and do everything he told me. I was not his puppet anymore! He didn't give a shit about Saskia; she was one of his little playthings, and someone he could manipulate to do whatever he wanted in return for a bit of "coke"! The night was dragging on and my fuse was getting shorter and shorter. I couldn't bear to hear much more of the shit he was dishing out. My mental silence was broken.

"Shall we play some dance music Christian?" He laughed as he walked over to his sound system turning the volume up and flicking on a cd

"Dance for us Christian, like you like to dance. Dance how you danced when I first saw you. I am sure Saskia wouldn't mind" he added.

"I don't think so Niko – you have had all the dancing sessions you are going to get from me!" I replied.

"Maybe you can dance with Saskia and I can WATCH you both! You are up for that aren't you Sask?" He said laughing as he did when he was imagining some disgusting perverted thought.

"GET UP AND DANCE FOR ME YOU WHORE!!" he screamed pushing her. She jumped up and started to stand. As I watched I was in total disbelief, she was going to do as he said!

"DANCE BITCH!" he shouted even louder, laughing. I had enough!!!! I stood up with such a force I knocked the chair I was sitting in over falling with a bang!

"Why don't you leave her alone Niko!" I shouted and in reaction he pushed his shoulders back and stood up. Normally this would have sent the fear of God through me but no more! I had had enough! Nothing was going to stop me now. It was the right time. I gathered my thoughts and worked out what I was going to say to him. Before I could open my mouth he antagonised me even more.

"You have something to say eh! Christian?!" he began

"Come on tell me what you have to say. You stand up for this girl like she means something to you! She's a nothing! A NOTHING!" he roared

"She gave birth to your son you sad fuck!!! Doesn't that mean anything to you?" I had to say it. This emotion had been building up and now was time for me to fly. He flew towards me his hands grabbing the lapels of my shirt.

"How the fuck do you DARE to speak to me as you do – you were a fucking nobody – you DARE to shout at me!" He was on one now his face red like a baboon's backside. Saskia had retreated to a corner in the room. She knew not to get involved in one of our fights. The music was blaring so I couldn't hear her too well but her contorted face and tears streaking down her face I could tell how upset she was. I stared into Niko's eyes and my eyes darted from his to his hands, you could never tell what he was going to do next. To put it mildly I was in fear for my life, however, we tussled each other Niko still ranting.

"I'll tell you who you fucking are shall I? – you ungrateful little shit!" he screamed at me hands bouncing off my chest. I grabbed his shirt and just clung on.

"Christian! Get me out of here I want to go" Saskia cried out. With the music as loud as it was Saskia screeching like a banshee the noise was getting too much. It was at times like this I would have liked my deafness back, but now that I was able to hear I had to take it on the chin and deal with it.

"LET GO OF ME NOW!!!!!!! I TELL YOU!!!!" I screamed in his face and stared right into his eyes, meaning every word and emotion that was coming out of me. He let go of me and swaggered around laughing his head off and taking more coke and having another brandy.

"Christian! I love you!" he cried at me breaking down in a heap at my feet.

"I would have given you everything, everything you ever wanted" I was angry now – how dare he speak to me about love after everything he had done. I was getting madder and madder my blood coursing through my veins as if on a relay race. He treated me so cruel. His words ran through my brain and just reiterated to me how he was such an evil person. He wasn't going to get away with anything now he was going to get his just deserts. I pushed him away but as I did so we both fell into the coffee table. He wasn't going to let go and neither was I.

"You know who I am Christian – you know who I am!" he shouted.

"Yes! I KNOW WHO YOU ARE – you are a fucking bastard of a man and I fucking hate you and everything about you" I screamed back, gritting my teeth as I did so.

"Yes Christian!" he said as he let go of my shirt falling to his knees once again and sobbing. What a sight he looked

"I am a sad man" he said lowering his voice in what one could take as shame. I looked down at him and he looked at me saying in a calm voice

"Christian! I am your father! I am your FUCKING FATHER!!" he yelled. I stood still not able to move a muscle and my heart skipping a few beats and tears welling up in my eyes. What did he say? I questioned myself. This was a fucking nightmare! What did he say? My fists hanging by my side, I clenched my fingers together and in what seems almost like a slow motion I lifted my arm and smack! I hit him square in the face, bloodied nose running down his face. I had started and I wasn't going to stop for anyone. This was my one chance to get him out of my life and the lives of those I cared about. He hit the floor.

"YOU LIE!!!!" I screamed at him fists clenching so hard my nails were biting into my palms. Saskia was screaming as loud as she could for me to stop

"Christian! NO MORE! PLEASE STOP!" she cried at me begging me to stop. No way! This was it.

"Christian I tell you the truth, you ARE my son!" he followed. I hated him but now I hated him twice as much. I pushed him to the floor sitting astride him holding him down; I reached across to the table and took the bag of cocaine that was to hand. One hand around his throat using my thumb to lower his jaw, as it lowered him still screaming, I poured the bag of cocaine down his throat until he was choking, then I pushed his jaw back up and put my hand across his nose and mouth so he couldn't breathe. His arms and legs flailing around like a man fighting for his life! This was long time coming and it had to be me to do it.

All the coke went down his throat I stayed sitting on his chest until his flailing stopped and it seemed like he had relaxed. He laid there in my arms dead. The room quiet and Saskia inching her way over to make sure the bastard had gone. Her tears still running and the odd sob coming from her every now and again. I leant over him tears dropping from my eyes like raindrops from a cloud. I felt sick. I looked at him my tears hitting his face and with each drop a small amount of white powder flew into the air. I was hurting so bad. Here I was looking down on this man who I had loved so much and who had given me my hearing back. I felt pain very deeply, we had the best of times we had the worst of times and now I was looking at my father. My head was fucked up and it all became too much. I let go of him and he dropped to the floor lifeless.

"Saskia! Get your things and get in the car NOW!!" I screamed at her. She got up so fast and grabbed her bag and cigarettes and ran out of the house to the car. I grabbed his wallet and my smokes and left. I stopped at the door and took one last long pitying look at him.......My father.... GOODBYE!!!!!!!!

I got in the car rather hastily and Saskia was sitting in the passenger seat shaking, make up running down her face, blood coming from her nose where she had been snorting coke with Niko. She did not look pretty now!

"Now when I drop you home you go in and act as normal as you can, just as if nothing had happened, you got me?" I said holding her face in my hands.

"Yes!" She said trying to catch her breath and shaking all the while her hands clasped round the handles of her bag as if she was on a "white knuckle" ride at the fun fair.

"You wait for me to contact you ok? And you tell NO ONE! DO YOU UNDERSTAND ME SAKIA!" I said holding her by the shoulders and making her realise just how much I now depended on her.

"YES! YES! YES!" She said as if I was getting on her nerves. I drove home at a sensible speed, so as not to draw attention to us. I dropped her off at her mother's house and returned to Gio's. The time was 2am and the house was still and dark. I walked into the lounge and looked up at the moonlight, reflecting not only on the fight Niko and I had just had, but the biggest shock I had received was that Niko was my father! I had to know the truth and there was only one person who could tell me the whole truth……..Mama!

CHAPTER 15

LAID TO REST

_____

I think I lay on the floor for about two days. I lost all track of time. I think I vaguely heard the phone ringing but I am not too sure. I hadn't washed or changed my clothes from that awful night at Paradisia. I think I could have filled an ocean with the amount of tears I cried. I screamed over and over as loud as I could

"WHY ME NIKO!? WHY ME?" I hit the walls and floor leaving blood trails where I had hit them so hard I had broken the skin on my knuckles. I was not going to forget these revelations quite yet. I had to have answers. The only person who could give those answers was Mama. I think I must have drunk two bottles of brandy and smoked about 1000 cigarettes. The world was passing me by in a haze but I had to do something. I paced the floor from end to end. Gio was away at this time and I could have done with him by me, but I was not going to interrupt his work. I missed him very much but was glad in a way that he wasn't there. I felt dirty! So fucking dirty! I could feel Niko's hands crawling over me and I began to reach to vomit. I had been sleeping with MY OWN FATHER!!!!!! How sick was that! I had contemplated cutting my wrists but Luis came into my head so I thought better of it. A realisation struck me! Luis WAS MY BLOOD BROTHER! This couldn't be made up I thought. I felt the need to go and see Mama. She would know the truth behind Niko. I grabbed my car keys and made my way to Mama's house.

Every one would have heard by now that Niko was dead. Nobody was knocking on my door and Saskia kept away as she had been told to do. Mama was sitting in her kitchen when I arrived.

"Ah! Christian my boy! Where have you been?" She said throwing her arms around me. "I have been ringing and ringing you but you no pick up the phone. Why not Christian, why not? Your Mama she worry for you" I shrugged off her touch and took a step back.

"NO! – DON'T TOUCH ME!!!" I screamed at her pushing her arms away as she stepped towards me a quizzical look on her face.

"Christian! I have heard……." She tried to continue but I cut her down.

"SHUT UP! SHUT up! For once please just shut up and listen!" I said to her. I was not messing around now. I had things I needed to know and I was not going to fall into her arms if she had known the truth of my parentage and had kept it from me. I couldn't look her in the face. I turned away as I said to her

"Who is my father Mama?" when I had asked the question I turned around and looked in her eyes. They could not lie to me.

"I demand you tell me!" I yelled

"TELL ME WOMAN FOR FUCK'S SAKE!!!" I was loosing my temper now. She looked scared and held her hands together and hung her head

"Please Christian" she begged as she began to cry "It does not matter I raise you Christian, I your Mama!" she clung to my arm. I could see the pain in her face but this did not take away the fact that she knew who my father was.

"TELL ME!!!!!" I yelled again! She sobbed frantically and collapsed onto the sofa.

"No! Christian, it does not matter now. Please Christian. Her pleading was getting beyond a joke now. The red mist descended and I lifted my arm and put my hand around her throat and shouted at her again

"TELL ME BEFORE I FUCKING KILL YOU!" I said shaking her

"NIKO!....NIKO!!!!!" she shouted "Niko" and I relaxed my grip and flung her to the floor she lay there looking up at me her tear stained face pleading with me to listen

"You are MY son – come back Christian" she said as I walked to the door. I stopped looked back with utter disgust and said to her in a calm but stern voice

"You are NOTHING to me" as I spat in her direction. I pulled the door open and stormed out slamming it behind me. As I walked to the car all I could hear were her hysterical cries for my return. I HATED her and I was NEVER going back. I never did return to that house and I never saw Mama again. Between Niko and Mama they had made my life one long drawn out lie. My whole existence was a lie. *"May they both rot in hell"* I said to myself. They deserved each other.

It was just like a local holiday. The shops and stores all had their shutters up and nobody was on the street. It seemed as if the whole village was still. Everyone would be attending the funeral. Villagers, shop owners, all types of important business man and heads of families crowded into the small local church awaiting his arrival, the music playing quite quietly. Greek Orthodox funerals were an elaborate affair with the entire community attending. Each person felt as if it was one of their own families that had passed.

If I was still at Paradisia his body would have been displayed in the home prior to the funeral and female relatives would have come to dress the body and sung lamentations. But he did not have that satisfaction. There was no way I was going to have anything to do with him, not after his revelations. So his body was left with the local mortician and this was fast becoming the norm for Greece and many of the old traditions were now dying out. The business took care of his funeral I just had to show up and introduce who I really was. Knowing how many people he had helped and the high standing he had in the community; the business showed some compassion and given that he wasn't having a traditional funeral they let the villagers take over the arranging. Little did they know what kind of man he REALLY was! It was up to me to show them as he certainly did not deserve their respect. Hopefully, after I had finished his name **would** be shit!

Traditional Greek funerals were a flamboyant affair with wreaths woven out of marjoram and placed on the graves of the loved ones. They served as prayers for the deceased in their future lives. The scent of the flowers mainly made of orchids, roses and beautiful carnations would waft up on lookers' nostrils and were so pungent. The ancient Greeks believed that at the moment of death a person obtained a higher level of consciousness. It meant that the last words uttered by a dying person were to be taken seriously. His last words to me were "I am your father!"

His funeral was a mixture of tradition and modern. Before the start of the procession the village church bell rang out its melodious knoll. The bells summoned the priests and the entire population of the village. It was led by non-relatives carrying offerings. The next in line was the Cantor (the priest who sang the scriptures). The procession for him went on its way but I was not one of them. As I looked around the people there waiting for the service to begin I noticed a mixture of traditional costume which was worn by the older women of the village, all in black and with shawls around their shoulders and covering their heads; and the modern day clothing that the youngsters wore. The men had their black arm bands on as a sign of respect for him; they would wear them for forty days. I was NOT going to wear one. I held no respect for him anymore. I wondered why there were so many people in attendance, they didn't really like him as a person they were in fear of him and bowed to his every wish. Everyone knew of our relationship but one thing nobody would expect me to say was that he was my father. There were certainly going to be a few people shocked by my revelation. The money lavished on the funeral and all the wealth that lingered around was outstanding really. There seemed to be so many cars. Bentleys, Mercedes, Jaguars and Daimlers along with sports cars littered the car park like confetti. All manner of makes and designs that only money could buy were among them. The richest of the rich all gathered, kissing each others hands and hugs abounding. They stopped as I approached and bowed to me, did they know something I didn't? I wore my black Gucci suit with a black silk shirt, black tie and black patent shoes, so shiny you could see your face in them. My hair was gelled back into a pony tail and I wore my shades. I hadn't slept, eaten or shaved for the best part of the week leading up to this. The news I had received from him had killed me inside. I had to make my stand in front of these people. I wasn't there for him I was there for me!

The traditional Greek music started to play the villagers entered the chapel and found their seats. The sounds amazed me things I had never heard before; the rustling of the ladies skirts, the clapping of hands as the men greeted one another, the low rumble of the ladies chatting in disbelief at what had happened to him. I heard a few babies cry and a lone woman's sobs came to my ears. All these sounds seem to be intensified and brought me back to what was happening. I straightened myself up shoulders back and head held high, and walked behind his coffin being carried by some of the local business men. I walked slowly, every step echoing in the open roof of the chapel. The gold decoration seemed to shine with brilliance and twinkle with each step I took. I could feel all eyes on me, I continued at a slow pace behind the coffin, the whispers intensifying until I could almost not take anymore. Sometimes I wish I had never had the implant especially at a time like this. I was feeling so numb and afraid my heart was racing and I seemed to shrink as if I was trying to disappear, which I was really as there was no way I wanted to be here right now! My shades hid the tear stained angry and tired eyes that had resulted from a week of tears and the knowledge of what I was about to impart to the congregation. They say the eyes are the windows to the soul; the only soul I could see was that of the arsehole who was in the box! The inside of the chapel was beautiful, decorated in marble with gold running threw it and gold covered pillars holding the roof up. Above the ceiling was adorned with bosses of different heavenly beings, gold running here there and everywhere. The pews were laid out in the shape of a cross and underfoot lay a beautiful gold edged red carpet. The brass work which set off the altar and held painted icons was made of stylised crosses within circles. Even the lights around the outside of the sanctuary when put one on top of another made a cross within a circle. There was one light on either side of the spiral stairway which led up to the pulpit. The interior stained glass windows lined the wall through which shone rivers of different coloured sunlight into the chapel. He had put a lot of money into the building in his time so the lavishness of it did not amaze me. He had to have a burial as Cremation is forbidden by the Greek Orthodox Church believing that it was blasphemous to the soul and therefore a burial would be in order. If I had my way I would have cremated him and thrown his ashes to the four winds of the earth. I had told Saskia to stay well clear and not even dare to bring Luis. He was my TRUE brother now and I had to keep him away from the images which stood before me now.

After the priest had said all he wanted to say, and most of it was in Greek so I didn't fully understand half of it; most of my life hearing I picked up English and that became my preferred language, the priest turned to me and asked if I wished to say anything. This was my moment, the moment when I would shatter everyone's illusions of him.

My heart racing even more than the trip down the aisle, I took the stand and looked at all the faces before me. Some I recognised, some I didn't, but they were all there for a reason to say goodbye to the man who had helped them through bad times but who had taken most of their earnings in loans from him. Everyone showed deep respect and the chapel fell silent. You could have heard a pin drop! Things were about to change.....

"Thank you, everyone, for coming here today. I don't have much to say other than…." I held my breath paused and took a look at the sea of faces then I focused on Gio, he had come in late and waited at the back of the chapel. He nodded at me and then I felt stronger, I wasn't on my own now.

"Life is too short isn't it?" I said in a louder voice, all faces turned towards me

"I only found out a short while ago who my real father was and today I am standing here burying him." I paused again, the lump in my throat growing bigger and the pain in my chest stronger. Every one's mouth fell agape and I think pennies had started to drop. BANNGGG!!!! I hit the stand in front of me.

"YES MY FATHER – NIKO WAS MY FATHER!!" by this time the tears had started to fall from my eyes hidden behind my shades. The priest sensed I was not in a good way; he placed his hand on my shoulder and nodded. I had done what I set out to do and said what I wanted to say. I didn't give a toss about what any one of those people thought. Now they could really see what a cruel and evil man he really was. I walked out of the chapel head held high leaving the congregation in there; Gio followed kissed my hand and hugged me.

"NO GIO! Don't EVER do that again" I shouted as I fell upon him. He lit a cigarette for me and placed it in my mouth wiping away some tears. They could all kiss my arse but never Gio.

The villagers would have expected to see a Heroon at his head but he wasn't going have an elaborate monumental tomb, he didn't deserve it, so he had the cheapest option which was a communal grave called a Polyandreion. This was what paupers were put in or for people who had little money and were of insignificant value in the business world.

The cortege made its way to the burial. Shock showed on their faces when they found out that he was going in the communal grave. The priest laid pottery on top of the coffin it had the inscription "Jesus Christ conquers" written on it. It would have been eve better if it had said "Christian conquers" In my head it did! Then he lifted a handful of soil and threw that in too. The mourners soon followed suit but with flowers and fruit and singing lamentations. Immediately after burial water is passed round to everyone so they could wash their hands. The wake was usually held at the dead person's family home but in this case I had nothing laid on at Paradisia. I needn't have worried as the priest had already put on a spread of food for the mourners to enjoy.

An array of delights lay in the dining room. Tables arranged with flowers and food. All types of titbits and desserts; there was plenty of cognac flowing and Greek coffee. Various dishes of traditional Greek fare were arranged symmetrically on the table, enough for a banquet; Kolyva (a ritual food given at various stages in a funeral), Paximadia (this was toast cookies made from almonds nice and sweet and just right for biscuit dunking)), many varieties of cheese, traditional fried fish with salad and the famous olives which was the backbone of the family business, all this food had been provided at great expense.

There was an old custom in which after a body was dead for one, three or seven years it was exhumed; it was examined and if it was found that the flesh had completely disappeared then the bones would be washed in wine and re-interred, however, if the body was black and putrid it was believed that the dead person had become a revenant which is to say they rose from the dead and haunted people who had either killed them or just to haunt their families. The pagan response to this to decapitate the individual or remove the heart or the usual ending these days is cremation. Even though this was a pagan custom it is revered to this day by the Greek Orthodox Church. Well what was the point of exhuming him we all knew he had gone to hell; he was master of it and had gone home.

Later Gio told me that Mama was ill. It was her ongoing heart condition; she had weakened and was now confined to her home. I changed the subject straight away. I didn't want to hear it I had just buried Niko.

Paradisia was mine and as soon as I could I was going to put the deeds in Luis' name. He asked about his father many times and I just said he was a star up in the sky and when we all died that's where we went. He accepted that. If Mama had been fit enough she would have gone to his funeral not out of respect for Niko but to beg forgiveness from me. She wasn't going to get anything out of me like Niko to me she was dead!

Life went on. I had a dance studio to run, a house to run. I also had the family business to tend to and lots of pies to sample and taste. People visited the house to pay their condolences and also to show respect for me as the head of the business that was helping them. I got into the swing of the business pretty easily as having lived with Niko I had learnt a bit more than he thought I did.

Mama passed away two months after Niko. She suffered a massive heart attack and I think that my rejection of her broke her heart, literally killing her. But she had lied to me all my life and this I could not forgive. I trusted her with my life and she betrayed me.

I have purposefully not called him by his name in this chapter as he did not deserve a name. He did not deserve life.

I had to learn how to take over everything he had left behind. I had to go to endless meetings and sign reams and reams of papers. The people of the village started smiling at me and nodding their heads. Gifts; lavish gifts at that, were sent to the house along with food of all different varieties. Without anyone saying anything I could tell they were happier that he was gone. It gave me a wealth that I had never known and travelling would now play a huge part in my life.

CHAPTER 16

UK

I had booked in at the perfect hotel in Soho in London. It was
a quiet and small hotel; I think one would call it compact
and bijou accommodation. (Ha! That's putting on an English
accent!!)

I could get all my dry cleaning done; there was room service
24 hours a day. The room I was given looked almost as if it had
been two rooms once, and modifications had made it into a
sleeping room with an en suite bathroom, shower included. I
had heard that English people were not very clean, but maybe I
had been told wrongly. The décor in the hotel was given a great
deal of attention and looked very nice for what I was paying;
it kept its period features and had classic elegance and style.
My room was very large for one person, I didn't see the point
in having all this space just for me but I guess it was all about

what credit cards you had and what car you drove. The staff was unobtrusive but they were helpful nonetheless and very friendly.

The location was great and the weather! Well what can one say? It was awful, just as I had been told it would be. Wet, damp and miserable, no wonder the British walked around with a long face half the time.

It felt very private here but was central to all the night life. It didn't feel like a hotel really more like a cosy inn, with no long corridors just little alcoves each housing a door with a brass handle. I would stay there again that was for sure, and they had shown me great respect as Niko had stayed there many times and was greatly respected by the management and they carried on that respect with me. London was THE best place to shop and it wasn't long before I was out trying things on and shopping until I dropped.

The hotel was within walking distance of the West End. The English have a very proud way when serving their clients in their shops and treat you almost like royalty. Getting fitted for a suit was quite hilarious especially the first time you buy one. The tailor said to me "What side do you dress sir?" I didn't know what he meant but another customer who was also having a fitting explained what he meant. It was what side my penis and testicles hung, this was so the suit could be fitted exactly as every man is different apparently! This did make me chuckle but it soon became part of my everyday life, as I was now able to afford the best and if that is what a tailor needs then that's what he gets.

Also the West End was the place in London where all theatrical people worked. There were many famous theatres here and I wanted to see as many of them as I could. The West End was surrounded by green spaces such as Regents Park (where they had a zoo), Green Park and probably the most famous of them all Hyde Park. I was in the UK and I was going to take every opportunity I could to soak up the atmosphere and see if I could do any business with the Brits. Many famous landmarks were there for all to see, the statue of Eros in Piccadilly Circus, the red double decker buses, the black cabs, Nelsons column in Trafalgar Square. The shopping in London was heavenly, walking up and down Regent Street and Oxford Street, the hub of British fashion. It looked like a mini New York with all the hustle and bustle of people rushing here there and everywhere. The only things missing were the yellow cabs and the street vendors selling warm pretzels and hot dogs. This was a step up to what I was to experience when I got to New York. The people here were very reserved and relatively quiet unless you were out on a bender and then you saw another side to the British. I got to know a few people whilst I was there and once you got to know them the British were not a bad lot really. There were pockets of people that were kind and generous and expected nothing but friendship and respect. On first appearance they would appear "stuck – up" but spending a few hours in their company you realise that people all over the world are not really any different to those back home. I knew I would learn to enjoy the trips I was going to take and the people I would meet and become close with this was truly the beginning of my life.

I wasn't in the UK just for fun though. Since Niko's death there had been some family business that needed dealing with and as his successor I was the one to sort it out. I had to tread carefully though as these people were new to me and I didn't know how they handled certain situations. Money and reputations were always at stake when it came to business. I had begun with Greece and I was working my way round the world. I would eventually circumnavigate the world, what an achievement for a back street boy who was deaf. I had come a very long way. I had arrived in the UK would sort out business here then make my way to the one real place I wanted to visit. Now I had my opportunity. I would be going to New York. People knew I was coming and the lavishness of my position was laid on no expense spared. I was being treated like a Prince. I wasn't going to turn any of it down either.

I was due to meet a couple of business men in a restaurant to talk over contracts and money and I was really looking forward to it. The gentlemen had already made it clear that I was an easier person to talk to than Niko ever was. That may have been so but I certainly wasn't going to be a pushover and they would see that I had my own mind. I was quite smart when it came to business as I had learnt a lot from Niko, and I knew a good deal and certainly knew when a deal was a bad one. One of the businesses I was involved in was cage fighting. Up until now I had only watched it and had learned that Niko owned a cage fighting club. This appealed to me and I had every intention of getting full involved in it.

The first time you see a professional cage fight, you may feel shocked. The fighters are capable of extraordinary aggression; fighters are often knocked out and sometimes suffer gory cuts and head wounds. They may dislocate a shoulder, or break something. Brutality is undoubtedly one of the sport's selling-points. Each fight is a journey into the unknown and provides an insight into how much the body can take.

I attended my first cage fight at an arena in London. It was a well attended event too with many top business men wagering on their favourite fighter. I had learnt to deal with fights when

I worked at Adonis and at the nightclubs I attended, so I was no stranger to brawling. I had learnt to take a long hard look at people and studied their body language; this was the first weapon against fighting. Read your opponent and you get the upper hand. I had a few fights and was usually compared to a bare knuckle fighter or street brawler. This was going to be different though, and I was really looking forward to being in that ring. There are many different types of moves in cage fighting some were mixed martial arts combined with the different disciplines of wrestling and boxing. There are few rules making as true to a real fight as you can get. It certainly isn't for the faint hearted but its not as violent as it looks, the main reason being that the fighters would rather submit than fight to the end. It was one of the sports that the media jump on because they can play on the violence, which is a shame because if they could see what was involved in the sport and the technicality of it, they would probably change their minds about it. It is a sport and it has violent elements. So does football and hockey. It's rather like a chess game when the guys get in the ring and fight you begin to understand exactly what they are doing and can sometimes work out their next move before they do it. It's like a beautiful dance. I think it makes the fight a lot more interesting when you stand up and do crazy stuff.....my favourite move is the Superman punch or the Jumping Elbow. I would show no mercy I wondered *"Would I have enough ice water in my veins and take out the other guy?"* I started giving the idea of fighting myself a great deal of thought would go into it but I had the feeling I could enjoy it.

The cage was there for safety reasons, to stop the men falling out of the ring. My first fight was in an Octagon. It was about twenty feet in diameter with two doors and painted black. I wore no protective gear, no one did. The guy I was up against was called Beppe. He was an Italian Stallion, known for his fighting prowess and his stamina. Even though he was about 40 years old he was still a fit man as fit as if he was only twenty years old. The bell rang and the fight started.... The first one to hit was Beppe he launched a left hook at me and got me square on the jaw on the right hand side, I started seeing stars. WOW!!!! Did he have a punch! He knocked me around quite a bit and I ended up with a few bruises. I was a little shaken only because I didn't expect him to hit so hard but once I had regained my composure he was going to see Mr. Nasty Mayirou.

The bell had gone for the second round and I was not going to let him get the better of me this time. I stood my hands assumed the position for my defence. I jumped a little on my feet, just lightly up and down to psyche myself up. He was doing the same, looking at me with pure hatred in his eyes. He thought he was tough, he hadn't seen anything yet. He got me quick in the first round but now I was watching his every move even the way his eyes moved, I transfixed my eyes on him. We shuffled back and forth just goading each other for a few seconds then WHACK! I planted my right fist firmly on to his mouth. I followed with a left hook to his ribs and a couple of shots on his chin, before concentrating on whacking his now bleeding nose and spreading it across his face. Three minutes later, his face was spewing blood like a broken hose pipe.

The crowd went wild all screaming at the top of their lungs, waving their arms in the air and screaming for me.

"CHRISTIAN!!! CHRISTIAN!!!" They screamed. The atmosphere was electric and they were shouting for me. I felt wonderful. The bell went ding ding and the normal blonde bimbo in a pair of skimpy shorts and a tight fitting bra top, would climb into the ring, the plaque for the next round waving above her head as she walked round in her high heels every muscle showing with each movement she mad. I danced around him back and forth the crows went, I played tactics with him making him think I was a fool but I knew what I was doing and I was certainly not going to let him win! I wanted the fight to last a bit longer than two rounds so I played with him for a while, making him dodge my lunges. We ended up on the floor a few times and he got me in a head lock with one of my legs in the air! Yes let me describe it to you, I didn't think you would know what I was talking about. He had hold of me on the canvas on my back he crouched over me he pulled my left leg up and held it in the twisted position and then he yanked my head towards him in a headlock. Pretty painful I can tell you but I managed to roll us over and get out of it. The ideas of prolonging the game was to let the crowd see you, build up a rapport with them and they would be behind you all the way, they would remember you and also the other heads of families attended and it was well to get in with them. Heavy money lay on these fights and big money was changing hands too.

Round three came and I was not going to pussy foot around anymore. So far we had only traded punches and had a bit of a roll around on the canvas. It was time to start using my kicks and use my knees and elbows. I was going in for the kill. I need to get him on the canvas instead of him getting me, only once mind you, only once! My goal was to get him prostrate on the canvas and "ground pound" his face into the canvas. I felt almost gladiatorial standing in that ring. I was fighting for the Roman Empire and demeaning the audience as I went. The first time you attend a cage fight you will be in shock as it is so bloody but it actually looks worse than it is. There would be extraordinary aggression. I had already cut Beppe's mouth and dislocated his shoulder. As I ran in to finish him off the doc tor stepped into the ring and put an end to the fight. Beppe looked at me and the unspoken words were *"I am going to finish this one day!"* I just smiled.

One evening I remember very well. It was a Friday night – cage fight night, and it could be a big win for me. I was asked to join a few people who were going to a disco bar afterwards for a celebration. I decided yes I would go. There was another side to me that people hadn't seen as yet, and it was good to relax sometimes in different atmospheres. I had been to this bar before. It was a nice adult place, no kids hanging around if you know what I mean. Being gay was a taboo subject amongst cage fighters, boy were they in for a shock! There was the exception – me! I never hid the fact that I was gay all my life and I was very proud. Some of the guys were closet gays and could only relax in my presence, they became themselves and those who didn't approve just kept their mouths shut, they knew better.

"Vodka and Coke! Please" I said to the barmaid behind the bar. She fluttered her eyelids and smiled, I offered a smile back. My attention came to the guy in front of me – *"Nah! It couldn't be!"* I thought but not daring to say out loud, NO WAY! I was seeing things.

"TJ!?" I said. "Is that YOU!?" I asked. It grabbed his attention and he turned around to face me. FUCK ME!!!!!! You could have knocked me down. There before me stood my brother TJ. The brother who disowned me for being gay! The same brother who had not spoken to me since I was fifteen years old!

"Hello Christian!" he said. WOW he had changed, he had aged a little. His hair was gelled back as normal and he wore greyish facial stubble. He had a deep scar under his left eye and both his ears were pierced. I couldn't believe what I was seeing, was this REALLY TJ?

"I had heard you would be in here tonight, so I thought I would pay a visit." he went on. "I do a bit of cage fighting myself sometimes" he continued. I was absolutely gobsmacked. With my jaw almost down to my chest I wondered what had happened to him along the way.

"You're looking good Christina!" He always called me that from the moment he found out I was gay. But I took that name with love I knew he was only joking. We chuckled "And doing very well for yourself I see" He carried on. I was the one who was in amazement, he just took my success as something he would expect from me, but my amazement was plainly obvious to the onlooker. He knew more about me; obviously, than I did about him. I guess I was too wrapped up in my own world. As we stood there talking for a few moments a tall guy walked over to us and stood beside TJ.

"Oh! By the way this is Yanis, Christian. Yanis this is my brother Christian" I said and we shook hands. "Christian this is my husband Yanis" I didn't think my jaw could drop any lower! Too see him in here was shock enough, I never thought I would see TJ in a gay bar; I never ever in my wildest dreams would have guessed that TJ was also gay! The grief that he gave me when I came out, he was positively cruel to me. He used to spit at me and generally be verbally abusive and there he was! Right in front of me standing arms locked with his HUSBAND!!!!!!!!! Well you could have blown me down with a feather!

"FUCKING HELL!" I screamed. At that moment I thought that maybe he was horrible to me as he was having a battle within himself about his sexuality and he couldn't cope with the stress of it. He looked so much happier now. I was happy for him. The rest of the evening was fantastic. I proudly introduced my brother to everyone and also introducing my "brother in law!" I was so happy. Yanis was a Corfiot and they had known each other for some time. They had been married for two years and had adopted a little girl called Sarah. Life had changed so much for TJ he looked very happy and content about what he had.

"I am sorry Christian for the past" he said

"Forget it TJ!" I said in return.

"Why do you cage fight? Are things that bad?" I asked him

"Let's say its easy money" he said with a little chuckle. He was back in my life. I felt a little more safe and secure.

I saw a great deal of TJ during that week in which we spent time both alone and with his new family. Sarah was adorable, blonde, blue eyes beautiful and very spoilt! (Like someone else we know). His husband Yanis was very camp and feminine, he whined on like a wife would do but he definitely idolised TJ. TJ obviously didn't feel the same as he was playing around on Yanis big time, he would say he was out earning and Yanis had to accept that no questions asked.

I decided that when I was done in the UK I was going to ask TJ, Yanis and the baby to come back to Corfu with me. I had a job for TJ that would keep them in the standard of living they were used to.

I had the shock of my life on the last Friday I was at the cage. My brother was fighting; he hadn't told me anything about it so it was quite a surprise when I saw him in the cage. He was fighting that night for his freedom. This was his passport out of UK. The earnings would pick up enough to buy outright a nice little place back home in Corfu. He had obviously refused my offer of a cash gift and said he wanted to earn it himself, he felt more of a man that way. The fight was getting intense and I was watching him pulling hair and biting and then he just exploded. He went vicious he head butted and punched him till the guy was on the floor dazed and heavily bleeding. He won his money that night and Yanis' heart even more so. They were coming back home with me. I was very proud my empire was growing stronger and now with my brother by my side I felt safe.

You know how close TJ and I were when we were growing up and how he disowned me when I "came out"! Its too funny how life turns out isn't it. One minute I was deaf and the next I could hear. One minute I was poor – the next extremely well off. One minute a car was in my dreams – the next I owned four. Who can ever predict where we'll be in the next hour……. Well meeting up again with TJ was like one minute no brother, gone for good and the next it was like we had never lost a day.

TJ was still very much the roamer and chancer. He still fancied everything in a skirt and pair of trousers. At the moment thinking of TJ it took me back to some very wonderful memories. The afternoon we were both travelling on a plane and high up in the sky. He gets off with this guy in a suit in the toilets. Oh my God! He had no shame.

After we got off the plane they ignored each other! TJ always loved the challenge I think and I envied him a little there. I'd often wished my challenges were a little easier! Three days after seeing that guy on the plane he had crabs!!

Fighting had always been in our blood since we were kids. Apart from family scraps we didn't fight each other but if anyone in our village or adjoining villages gave us reason to we would give a few people a fight they weren't expecting. Now we were both involved in the caging, we had shared some fights in the cage too – again against others wanting to take us on. TJ was fighting when I'd first met up with him again in New York City and I was in the predicament that I didn't have to fight, I actually owned fighters of my own, then I went on to own TJ. I had done it in a way so I could handpick his fights. This way I could also protect him too and he could earn himself good money. We oozed off each other when we were as you would call a "tag team". Those old moves we learnt years ago in Greece served us well in New York and we ravished on it. We were fighting the Miraz brothers one night, they were well known on the circuit and they cam from France. They were the same build and age as us too funnily enough and we never had seen them fight live before. God they were fucking good! The oldest of the two kicked shit out of TJ in the opening round and it was only when I realised then that they were serious. We were going to have to fight our bollocks off to survive.

My brother had been pulverised. He was punched senseless but I couldn't get close enough to "tag" him. I was hungry to fight and I was fuming to see TJ getting such a beating. It was my turn now and I was going to avenge my brother's name. I already had the next two rounds planned in my head, I mean a business man is always planning ahead so it didn't hurt to prepare. I would have to fight them one by one, they were too strong together and they were dirty fighters too. I stayed away from the youngest Miraz for a little while when the round opened just toying and playing and when I estimated there was about a minute left I changed tactics. I started to throw some really hard punches in. It took four solid full frontal punches to his chin and mouth area to put him on the floor. My knuckles hurt a little and I had inherited a cut probably from his teeth. As he hit the floor I passionately kicked him to the head. So the final round started and I was to face the elder of the Miraz brothers who put TJ down. This was going to be a hard and tough fight. The crowd were like a pack of savage animals, jeering, shouting and singing. There was quite a greedy atmosphere in there.

In-between rounds you had a minutes cool off. Normally I just sipped water and that minute would go fast. TJ was standing in our corner, his eyes nearly shut as they were that swollen. The doctor on standby overruled TJ's desire to go back in to fight so the final round was left to me and the more I looked at TJ's face the more I was spitting razor blades. I would laugh out loud thinking *"What the fuck are we doing here and how did we get in this shit!"* I could see Mama getting in the cage grabbing us both by our ears and marching us out of the cage in front of hundreds of people swearing in Greek like she did! It's funny what you see when maybe your life flashes before your eyes. I had to fight like a bastard and fight like a bastard I did. He was so going to pay for what he did to TJ. TJ knew I was out to kill the Mirazs. I had the bit between my teeth now and God only could help them.

As we entered the centre of the cage he put out his hand to bang mine and I didn't retaliate, I just spat at his feet and the crowd's excitement exploded. I loved receiving the attention, being the person of stature that I was, especially in that place. The place was packed to the rafters with screaming fans all backing the one they wanted to win. Miraz was glaring at me as we got ready to fight but my glare was hungrier. I went at him a hundred miles an hour and he held no chance of coming out of this glowing. I went in with my fists just throwing punches where I could. On about the sixth punch blood was oozing from his mouth and nose which in turn covered my hands. Then a couple of swift punches to his stomach disabled him from lashing out at me for a while and gasping for breath he slowly sunk to the floor. I stood behind him and grabbed his hair and held on to it tightly in my fists. I held him there like a frightened animal pouring with blood and begging for mercy. I looked into the silent audience. They were all staring at me with baited breath. I stared hard at their faces and especially the highly respected and rich people all betting big money. I was the best they had seen in a while. I was number one in there and they nodded knowingly. I then turned and looked at TJ.

"For you" I mouthed to him and he nodded. I finished him and we won the fight. This is how close TJ and I were.

CHAPTER 17

KELSO

Browsing on the internet as I did quite a lot of the time, I came across this fantastic looking photograph of a really beautiful guy. His name was Kelso and we started speaking in a gay chat room. Kelso was an attractive man, in his early forties, he was six feet four inches tall and slim with piercing blue eyes. His blonde hair was very short and swept back. He was of Swedish/American descent and lived in the United States of America; I had developed a liking for yanks.

After a while everyone knew that Kelso and I had become an item. We spent hours together online and we began with the flirting process as one usually does. Firstly we made innocent eye contact on the webcam. Occasionally we would catch each others gaze and would make each others heart beat faster than normal and it wasn't long before the 'L' word was used between us. The natural thing followed with discussions of marriage and being together. Oh my god! He was extremely serious and I wondered how long this would last! I had only ever dreamt of going to America but now this looked like it was becoming a reality. I looked back on the times I had stood on Mamas balcony and looked out over the sea and wondered what life held for me. Now I was beginning a new life away from here. Yes I would miss my family, what there was left after Niko had destroyed everything I had ever known. I had only read about it at school in the geography and history books. I knew it was a vast country but it held many opportunities for a young man like me. The next morning I grabbed my rucksack, packed as much into it as I could. The bag was that packed the seams looked as if they were straining to stay locked together. I picked up my ticket and passport and made my way anxiously, but excitedly to Sportera airport. The plane was boarding at 8.30pm; the announcement had been made for all passengers to make their way to the departure lounge

"All passengers for flight no A173 to New York please make your way to the boarding gate with your passports and boarding passes ready! Please enjoy your flight!"

I was wearing a pair of tight denims with the knees and arse ripped out, so fashionable it was then. My Reebok trainers were spotless white with gold trim. And my white t-shirt was tight and showed off my masculinity to its almost best. While we waited in the departure lounge to board I phoned Kelso and we spoke of our feelings and where we would meet. He would be waiting for me at the arrivals gate. With security the way it was at the time I had to collect my luggage from baggage claim and then go through customs by myself. I actually went through with a clear conscience. Kelso told me that he would be waiting with Mel and Aston from downstairs with 100 balloons!

As I boarded the plane I felt nervous and scared but also very excited as this was a new opportunity for me in a new country away from all the crap that had happened so far. This was the first time I had ever left my homeland but what the fuck! What was I leaving behind? Let's face it Corfu had been rough and it was time for me to explore men like Kelso who were so different to the people I had been raised around. Greek men are dark skinned and most are hairy with sickening fluff in their belly buttons. Kelso was white and he was very different to anything I had known before. His accent drove me wild too and it took a long time for us to be really able to understand each other on the telephone but we laughed all the same. We shared many tender times and we shared many tears too. When we weren't on the webcam we spent many hours on the telephone and I am talking sometimes four, five, or six hours at a time. The telephone bills were astronomical. This was because the time differences between Corfu and USA were quite wide, seven hours to be exact. We would play music to each other endlessly and sometimes if I had been smoking dope I would burst into song singing the occasional love song down the phone with no shame as I couldn't sing but the words meant everything. Again, here you will notice that music still played a big part of my life and emotions and feelings were always tendered from words of a song and I could express my feelings through music, which funnily enough wore off on Kelso and he began to feel the music deeper than he ever had before. He knew he was going to be living with a teenager who liked loud music and would be dancing all over the place. He didn't seem like a man in his 40s he behaved younger and had energy he had SPUNK! You know that thing that only men have when they really love to do something. I liked his morals of being faithful and his honesty and communication were the things that bound us together little did I know it was going to be nothing like the fairy tale phone calls and cam sessions we had had for nine months.

The flight was very comfortable as I went first class, it was quite a long flight as it took twelve hours, but once we had landed it felt like no time at all. On the plane I was treated like royalty in first class. There was plenty of leg room and every service you could think of. I even got eyed up by one the male "trolley dollies", at one time I got the distinct impression he was giving me the come on to one of the restrooms to join the "mile high club". But I thought better of it I was on my way to Kelso and I would be more than happy with the service I received from him.

Before I knew it we had landed and were taxiing to the arrival gate. I walked through the tunnel to the main part of the airport in Detroit. I followed the signs to the baggage claim and then joined the rest of the passengers to go through customs, after I had collected my suitcase from the conveyor belt. I already had my rucksack as I had taken that on the plane with me. I managed to get through customs quite quickly, and as I went through the door there he was! I looked about nervously and caught Kelso jumping up and down like a ballerina waving the 100 balloons as hard as he could, just as he said he would when we talked while I was waiting to board the plane. Right beside him dressed in their finery were Mel and Aston. I stopped dead in my tracks and my heart also felt as if it had stopped. My eye caught Kelso's eyes and I saw how electric blue his eyes were as he fixated on me until I reached them. I shook every step I took my knees feeling as if they couldn't hold my legs up any more but I knew I had to get through this. We had found each other at last! I looked and broke into a large smile and all three broke into smiles too. There was uproar of guffawing at the top of our lungs drawing attention to ourselves. My steps became quicker as I almost ran towards them behind the barrier. Kelsos arms opened wide as I ran towards him I saw that look on his face that I had seen many a time on the web cam. It felt good and I felt safe. We were so happy to meet after all this time being linked only by the internet. People milling around us meeting their own loved ones but who couldn't help themselves but looking at us. We must have been the noisiest ones there. We screamed as we each said hello to the next and the weird couple kind of broke the ice with a....

"OMG!!!! It's you! It's really you!" Compliments were being thrown at me left right and centre all with heavy American accents which I had come to adore over the time Kelso and I had been talking. Everything was a little daunting and overwhelming but we managed to make our way to the transport to take us all home to Kelsos house. Mel and Aston fought over my case each one trying to look better than the other. A right pair of Queens they were if ever I saw, but my! They were funny!!!. Kelso and I joined hands as we walked to the truck, Mel put my luggage in the back of the truck and we made our way home.

The house was a town house which was very modern. There were wooden floors throughout with white walls and a large cage in the corner. Inside the cage was a large parrot with beautiful rich colours of red, green and blue. He hopped up and down and the occasional word came out which we fell apart laughing as it was not something you would expect a parrot to say "GET THE PHONE! GET THE PHONE!" The garden was of a fairly medium size. It was big enough for sunchairs and loungers and a decked patio. The neighbourhood was overrun by Arabs walking around in the kaftans or whatever they are called.

In the basement of the house there lived Mel and Aston. Aston was an American drag queen and Mel his partner was Hispanic and was more or less Aston's slave fetching and carrying for him. Mel just stayed for the money and somewhere to live. He liked cleaning up and was immaculate in his approach to keeping the house clean for Aston. He was a fairly tall guy and was very muscular indeed. Just my type! He did have campness about him especially when he caught you looking at him. Mel worked at the local airport as some type of a manager and therefore always looked immaculate in his dress for the office in top of the range suits. My step-parent worked at the same airport and that is how Kelso and I got in touch over the internet. This was how we got to know each other and there was an instant attraction. We spent hours day and night talking and talking, sharing photographs and endless hours of seeing each other over a web cam. I do believe that Kelso first saw a picture of me too on a web page and he instantly contacted me. First we emailed each other and they grew longer and longer with each successive letter. During this time we became closer and I was actually dating Jay at the time so felt a little guilty, but Kelso and I sat down and chatted and we knew we had to tell the world the truth

It took me about three days to realise that maybe I had made a big mistake moving. Not to the States but to this house, it wreaked of debauchery. Newcomers to the house were subjected to an initiation ceremony. Whoever thought that up was really twisted. The first part of the test was to walk around the house strip bo1llock naked for the first twenty four hours of being in the house. NAH! Nooooooooo way was I going to do that.

"BOLLOCKS!!!" I shouted "I am not doing that!"

Mel and Aston said they had to do it when they moved in so why shouldn't I? Kelso sat there and grinned. I was not into any of this what I could only call weird shit!

One day whilst I was chilling out and trying to relax, listening to music was one of my most favourite things to do and I was always dreaming up new moves to the new music that was coming out. All of a sudden the music stopped and on came a song I had heard of. It was called "Someday" and was now blasting out of the speakers, I looked around to see what was happening and I saw Kelso dressed in a long black wig and a long black dress, and I was shocked to say the least but then out of his mouth came this god awful sound he was "singing" very loud. The bottom of my jaw dropped, I had never seen anything like this in my life. Yes gays were relatively open in Corfu and not many people batted an eyelid, and that was usually the old women dressed in their grieving weeds. I was dumbfounded with what I saw, I wouldn't have minded but he wasn't even very good. He took me to the pride festival one afternoon and that was very enduring. He dressed me in tight blue frayed denim shorts with beige caterpillar boots and that was it! I had a leash around my neck made of leather attached to his wrist. This was the most dynamic of celebrations of gay, lesbian, bisexual and transgender cultures living in the local community. My thoughts ran to the love that he had expressed to me but I began thinking that if he loved me as much as he said he did he would not have put me in this position. Being leashed showed everyone at the festival that I was his "boy"; his "dog" and that basically he owned my arse and nobody was allowed to touch. For fun value it could have been very good but he was making a serious statement and I was just his show piece. I can't say it was all doom and gloom and weird things going on though. He drove me all around his hometown and took me to everything that was going on or happening in his community. His home was minutes from Downtown Detroit and very close to the Metro airport, oh yes! Not forgetting the Henry Ford museum which was of interest to me as I loved cars and he was the first man to invent the motor car. The town was named after a national military hero in the 1840s and he became the twelfth president of the USA. I found the history quite interesting and was sucking it up as we went to all the historical places he could find.

We spent hours talking and listening to music. Just as I did he felt he could relate to music and that had happened in the time that we had talked to each other. I would often send him songs that meant something about our relationship. Jay had once said the same too, for some reason I had opened their eyes to the magic of music and dance. He worked a ten day shift and then had four days off which we spent most of the time in bed or around the house. He put a sign on the front door which said "DO NOT DISTURB – MEN AT WORK" because of this notice, nobody bothered us. He had the patience of a saint when it came to our sexual relationship as I was not at all comfortable or confident after the business I had been through with Niko. The pain he had caused me resulted in emotional scars and they deeply affected me. As long as the lights were on and I could see him I would be fine. We would just lie down together and kiss and cuddle for hours. I could not be versatile with him though, I was "Top Man" in this relationship if you get my drift, although he was very loving and attentive and gentle at all times, especially when we were alone.

After some time Kelso and I were having a few problems. He tried to be like a mixture of my father and my lover. I was a young man and I wanted to be treated like a man, this was not for me! He then wanted me to start dressing for him and shave regularly. He insisted on where he wanted me to be whenever he called. This was starting to become what I had left with Niko. I was no longer going to be someone's puppy dog. I was my own person and I would do what I pleased now!

He always wanted to be in control of me and show me off as if I was his trophy. I had been here before. I was required to sit on his knee in public and wear pretty pink ribbons in my hair. I often thought that I was going back where I was with Niko and I knew I had to make things different.

Another time Kelso was trying to imitate one of my favourite singers, I still joke with friends about this. He put on a sheer evening gown and wig whilst doing the vacuuming. I understand that people like to do this kind of thing; such as dressing up in drag to go to a nightclub, but Kelso was weird he wanted to dress in drag to do his housework. Was this guy for real? He wanted us to get married in Vermont and he was having custom made rainbow suits for the wedding. He wanted to take me to Providence town and walk me around on a leash just like a dog. I admit being a gay man and having fantasies myself, but Kelso was over the top. In fact his fantasies were so over the top he made a streetwalker look like a virgin.

I knew deep in my heart I didn't want to be with him for the rest of my days. I woke up early one Sunday morning and just left. I didn't leave any notes or call; I just left and went far out of sight. He didn't fit in with my fast and moving life, he just wanted to tie me down as his little toy boy and do for him everything he wanted. I wasn't going to be his bitch for the rest of my life, so I made the decision to travel a bit more and made my way to New York.

CHAPTER 18

NEW YORK CITY

Ah! New York City! Stepping off the plane at JFK airport I was very nervous. I had not been to New York before and it held many dreams for me. It was the centre of theatreland and I was hoping that I may be able to get some work here. I took a yellow cab to my hotel right on Time Square. I checked in to my room and the bell boy took my luggage for me, we went to the 16th floor left the lift and made our way to room 1632. I looked out of the window and took the sights in below. The hustle and bustle of every nationality you could imagine was scurrying about doing their business. The sun was shining and glistening off the windows of which there were many. I had never seen a tall building before let alone a million of them.

I took a walk to familiarize myself with the area and see if New Yorkers were as hospitable as they had been portrayed. The evening was dark but with the amount of lights on each building shining it truly did look like "the city that never sleeps!" I walked out of the hotel and ambled along the sidewalks listening to people as they chattered about all manner of things, their day at work, their love lives, and many other things. I reached the square and I noticed a crowd of people and one man in the centre yelling at the top of his voice and slamming a thick book in his hand. I made my way over to see what the commotion was about and saw a young black man shouting, I took a step back and listened to what he was saying, I could see many people laughing and then all of a sudden this middle aged woman went up to him through the crowd and said

"You can't tell people they are going to hell. What right have you to tell people they are going to hell?" and then she began quoting things from the bible and telling the man that he was very wrong to preach these things to people.

"Are you God?" She yelled.

"No!" he said and then she went on to tell him that only God is our judge and this man had no right to tell people that they were going to hell. If anything he would go to hell himself for preaching untruths. I smiled and left the group. I walked for what seemed like a lifetime. Each building getting bigger, at one point I leaned my head back as far as I could to see if I could see the top of the building. Then fell over as I would have had to lie on the sidewalk to get the full view!

New York City was a vast place, much bigger than my hometown in Corfu. The shops went on and on and everywhere you looked there would be a street vendor selling things like, pretzels, hot dogs and all manner of gifts for the tourist, of which there were many. After all who in their right mind wouldn't want to visit New York, it was the shopping capital of the world it seemed. Yellow taxis were everywhere; it was much easier to take a cab than walk or bus. All the cabbies knew where you wanted to go and were most obliging to newbies in New York. Whistles blew outside every hotel where the doorman would hail a cab for his patron. The roads seemed to be made on a grid pattern and it was difficult to get lost as New Yorkers were very polite and helped you find what you wanted. I got the impression they loved visitors to their state. The roads were crowded with not just the yellow cabs but long stretch limos and open top buses, which were mainly for the tourists. There were buskers on every street corner and painters outside the theatres asking to draw your portrait, people everywhere either there to make a fast buck or to just enjoy the lifestyle. The vast majority of people seemed very happy. I loved to people watch and I was soon able to discern a typical New Yorker as they tended to wear baseball caps white socks and they spoke very fast. Everyone seemed nice and polite and very often I would hear the phrase "Have a nice day sir!"

I spent the next day looking around the shops and found out just how cheap everything was. Clothes, trainers, and cigarettes were all half the price of what I was paying back home. Alcohol was a different matter. You had to be 21 to drink alcohol in the states but as I was a mini celebrity I could get a drink fairly easily.

Central Park was an oasis of green in the middle of all those huge concrete buildings. It was a beautiful place where you could rest or just have fun. Many, many joggers were running around with their headphones in their ears and each holding a bottle of water. There were main roads in the park where cars could be seen and rollerbladers getting their daily exercise. The park has over 800 acres of land. There is a zoo and an ice rink in the winter. Also a boathouse was located in the park and seeing the boats took me back to my hometown in Corfu. I went to the park for a while whenever I could, it was so peaceful and beautiful there I spent many hours just relaxing and people watching.

Greenwich Village wasn't that far from the hotel either and was a well known place to go for the bohemian culture. Located between Houston and 14th Street it was one of the few places in New York that lost the simple pattern of the grid laid streets of the main town. Coffee shops, jazz clubs, bars many restaurants and off road Broadway theatres lined the streets of New York. I had many a proposition whilst I patronized the gays clubs and night clubs, but I declined many offers as I was a dance teacher and was there to improve my skill so I had to behave. The spectacular neon signs that lined the streets were a real attraction for visitors. I had heard of the famous Times building atop which was a huge ball and at midnight on New Years Eve this ball was dropped with many onlookers waiting and getting excited about the New Year ahead. I had never seen it for real only heard about it but I was determined to be there at one time when the ball dropped.

West of 5th Avenue was the theatre district inhabited by professionals and amateurs trying their luck in making it to the big time! Many years ago it was the seedy area of New York and was full of strip clubs and peep shows, but when the theatre arrived they went to the backstreets. Many of the landmark theatres were restored to their former glory. Most of the great theatres were near Times Square and west of the Broadway. The theatre I had come to work had its own history which I found fascinating. It opened in 1910 and was originally named after Shakespeare's theatre in England. This theatre had a retractable roof to enable the theatre to stay cool and open in the summer. For nearly twenty years the theatre housed a variety of plays and musicals until 1932 when it was turned into a movie house. In 1958 the theatre was gutted by fire and was rebuilt in its present configuration as a legitimate theatre. It was renamed in honour of America's foremost husband and wife double act; it was an amazing place to work.

It was work time! I had received a contract to work backstage with a dance troop who couldn't get their shit together for a very big show. They would call on me at times when rehearsals were flagging. I would spend a few weeks working with them to try and perfect their techniques. It was extremely exciting and I was able to travel all over. It was coming to the end of rehearsals and the troop gave me a going away party to say thankyou. It was arranged that we meet in the local bar which was a "straight" bar and have a few drinks there before moving on to a club and partying the night away. We all got lagging drunk and went to one of the guys' condominium and rounded off the night with light banter and a smoke. The troop I had been teaching for the last three weeks had all got to know me over this short period of time and they knew which way my balls swung. They were a cool gang and not bothered by my sexuality.

By the time we had got to the club we were a bit merry and carried on the session by downing quite a lot of shots of tequila slammers and quervos. It was a good night and everyone seemed to be enjoying themselves. The club was swinging and the atmosphere absolutely pumping. There were lights everywhere you looked and mirrors all over the place, it looked like ooftahs paradise! Big glass chandeliers hung from the ceiling and the waiting staff running around like headless chickens with trays adorned with our next drinks. What looked like a banquet was laid before us full of pizzas, hot sausages and picky bits for us to nibble on, followed by large jugs of cocktails. Each glass was topped off with an umbrella and an olive in it. The night was seemingly rocking with many people dancing and laughing. The atmosphere was electric and we were all having a wonderful time. We all danced as a group and it was so nice to just be myself and not teaching. There were a few who tried to get me to perform.

"Come on Christian get up and show us what you can do!" Shouted Billy one of the guys encouraging all the others to jump on the bandwagon and get me dancing. Well you know me! I was never one to turn down an opportunity to perform. I began strutting myself on the floor, onlookers would have thought I owned the place the way I had commanded the attention of everyone. I was in the middle of the floor and everyone else on the floor stepped aside to give me room. It was like a mad house in there everyone a little worse for their drink but everyone enjoying their time. It made a great change to being dragged around the gay festivals I had attended with Kelso, there I felt owned, here was different I owned the dance floor. I let myself go and drew attention. This was when I was happiest. I had stopped and was congratulated by everyone watching. After I had spoken to them for a few minutes I asked them to join us and suddenly our party of fun loving dancers was increased to what seemed like ten fold. Dancing earned me respect and I was very pleased that they remembered me. I have to laugh because our party had suddenly got alot bigger and everyone wanted to be part of our little group, we were having such a great time.

The alcohol was reaching the parts others did not and made everything that was going on seem unreal. It's hard to explain, but I was having a really good time and I felt so mellow without a care. Smoke was coming out all over the place and bubbles were erupting from the ceiling – oh! It was really magical. What a great place to have a good going away send off. Well, it was getting closer to the time, chucking out time, so it was decided we would all go back to Megan's apartment. Megan was a 19 year old dance student and had a waitressing job to earn money to live and basically try and further her career. It cost money to go to auditions. She was about five feet ten inches and of slim build with gorgeous long blonde hair and blue eyes. She had been born in New York but had got herself into the drug scene. She was at one point very heavily into drugs, mainly cocaine and pills. Most of the dancers were taking it so it was readily available. She had cool neighbours so they didn't mind us having a little party back there. They were proper junkies so they were often out of it anyhow! We all walked back to her apartment, it wasn't far probably about 3 blocks away and when you are lagging drunk it all seems to not matter anyway. We were dancing in the streets, smiling at passers –by who were smiling back also under the influence of alcohol and whatever else they were taking.

There were six of us who went to Megan's. Besides Megan there was Johnnie who was a college kid of 19, and he had been trying his best to make his fortune in Broadway. He lived with his parents who were very well off but he was like the worst dancer in the class and he needed the help more than anything. Peter was a 23 year old dancer. He worked as a DJ and shared his apartment with his girlfriend Lea; she was a bit of a nutcase but made everyone laugh with her zany sense of humour. Lea was 20 years old and they both had long brown hair. They had been dating for 2 years and moved in together, when they left Arizona to come to New York. He was a really serious guy in the classes but as soon as he left the house he was a real party animal! I had been out on the lash with him before!

Shana was a skinny dancer and was very tall for a girl she measured six feet, or as some girls would say five foot twelve inches. Her appearance was a bit daunting as she looked as if she needed feeding up. She was a part time child minder and lived with her mother and younger brother in the slum area of the city. She was the other nutcase of the group and she could take her vodka shots – WOW! Then of course there was me. They had all been part of my dance troop though, and I had worked with them five days a week for three weeks, so we were all good friends. I would be sad to leave here and I would miss everyone. New York!....OH!...NEW YORK what a wonderful place you hold in my heart.

I sat and thought of the old days in the mountains in Greece where I had a small dance school just for the children of the village. Look where I was teaching now!

Megan's place was wild, decorated well with really vibrant and colourful paints. I couldn't believe I was really here, here of all places New York City the place for dancers and actors. The walls were mostly pink and yellow; I need my shades in there!!! The sofa was a bright purple and everything was in its place. She had beads instead of doors in most of the rooms, apart from the toilet which did have a door on it. Megan went to the music system and turned it on and music blared out of the speakers, next to come out was the alcohol. Oh yes! Fucking more consumption. Peanuts and crisps arrived from the kitchen and put in little bowls scattered around the room. Everyone hit the floor and began doing their drugs. I rolled a fine joint full of some really good weed that I had managed to obtain. Peter and Lea started to snort their white powder up their noses and the rest of us just smoked green. The booze flowed like honey from a hive. You could guarantee there would be some sore heads in the morning. I had no objection to people doing the drug of their choice but I have to say it did stir up some old memories for me and a lump developed in my throat. Watching all this powder disappearing put me in the mood to get very drunk, so that's what I did. I wasn't going to sink into a bout of depression, which was very easy to do, so I just had more drink and chatted to everyone who was there. Shana left pretty early she got in a yellow cab and off she went. Peter and Lea hit the sofa and got caught up in what one can only say was debauchery! We didn't want to see that so Megan politely told them the direction to the spare bedroom and off they went, not letting each other go for one second, kissing as if their lives depended on it. Johnnie flaked out on the bathroom floor and Megan just dropped a blanket over him. It left Megan and I just to sit and talk and have a drink and we managed to put a bottle of Vodka away between us, goodness knows how but we managed it! We continued drinking for about an hour; I remember laughing so much, we were having alot of fun. We made our way into Megan's bedroom and she began helping me off with my shirt, and I think I can remember her undoing the buttons on my denims but after that the rest was really a blur.

The morning came and the daylight shone through the curtains and onto my face. Damn! Where the fuck was I!? I rolled over and looked across the bed, for fuck sake!!!!!! Megan was in bed with me her hair long and draped over her pillow and. She had her back to me, Oh my God!!!! What was I doing in bed with Megan? I lifted the duvet a bit and even worse!!!!!! I was strip bullock naked. "SHIT! SHIT! SHIT!!!!!!!!" I thought to myself. I leapt out of bed and scurried to put on my boxers and jeans, just as I was buttoning them up I heard a rustling sound, my head lifted and I could see Megan stirring in the bed, she rolled over and said with a gleaming face

"Morning cutie!" the smile on her face told me something I didn't really want to know.

"Erm!! Yeah morning" I said very nervously and not knowing where to look.

"You got to go so quick Christian!?" She asked in a flirting manner, looking at the bed and inviting me back in. For God sake I couldn't remember what had happened the night before. Had Megan and I had sex? I know we slept in the same bed but it didn't mean we had sex. Did it!?

"I have to go Megan, sorry but I have lots to do" I hesitated and rushed putting the rest of my clothes on and running almost out of the door. I felt dirty, what the hell happened last night? I hailed a cab and went back to my dingy hotel room. I ripped my clothes off as fast as I could and jumped into the shower. I stood there for what seemed like a lifetime, the hot water beating down on my neck. I was in the shower for about 45 minutes; just letting the water run all over me as I was thinking about the possibilities of what had occurred the night before. I couldn't wash fast enough, I scrubbed and scrubbed with the loofah and made myself red and sore. The more I thought about what had happened the worse I felt. I could smell her all over me. She knew I was gay, she had taken advantage of me and I didn't know how I was going to explain things to her. She had basically fucked me when I was incapable of really knowing what I was doing. I had to get out of New York City now, I couldn't stay any longer. I wanted to go back home. I left there unfortunately not the way I had planned.

CHAPTER 19

MY GIRL

I was relaxing after a morning working out in the gym. I often went to the gym if I didn't have a class in the mornings. My mobile beeped, it was an unknown number but was a message reading "CONTACT MEGAN IN NYC ASAP!" It included the number I needed to ring. What the hell did she want after all this time? Maybe she wanted a holiday over in Greece or some work. Well whatever it was, it was important enough to leave me a message like this.

I finished dressing, grabbed a coke from the fridge and started walking out to the car. I dialled the number which I had received in the text message. It rung for quite a while before an answer phone cut in *"Please leave a message after the tone and I will get back to you!"* Bloody phone, a mobile phone is for answering not leaving a message on it. That's why it's called a mobile so you can have it with you wherever you go. This did not put me in a good frame of mind, I wasn't looking forward to speaking to Megan as it was and now I had her answer phone it was even worse. I left a message as requested

"Erm! Its Christian, I got your text, returning your call, I will call again tomorrow" and then I hung up. Jesus! I had not spoken to any of the dance troop since I had left New York.

As I had returned home I was now on Greek time and as there is a time difference of seven hours I waited until my afternoon, it would be morning in USA. I took myself off to the kitchen where Luis was eating his breakfast and Gio was getting the car ready to take Luis to school. I loved the mornings especially if I saw Luis smile; it started the day off good. He would kiss me goodbye and I would say to him

"Sagapo! My little brother, have a good day!" and he would always smile and whisper to you too. I had done all the normal things like showering, shaving and dressing. I made the beds and finally grabbed a cup of tea. I would make some toast and the music would be escaping from my music system, while that was blaring out I would do some washing and generally clean the house. It depended really on events the night before as to how much needed doing and what time I would get up the next day. The afternoon came quite quickly and I thought I would try and ring New York again. I dialled and it rang four times before it was picked up at the other end.

"Hello!" I hadn't heard her voice for a while and it made me feel a bit unsteady.

"Hi Megan! It's Christian" I replied waiting anxiously for her next words. It must have been quite serious as I couldn't think of any other reason why she should contact me with such urgency.

"OH MY GOD!" She said in an excited voice. "Wow it's been so long. Well thanks for calling me it means so much." She sounded a little nervous on the other end.

"Megan! Is you ok?" I asked as I thought this charade had gone on long enough.

"Well ok Christian it's like this you see. I am pregnant; the baby is due next month and erm…… You are the father without any doubt." The air was silent. "What! How! When!" I was in shock and couldn't believe what I was hearing.

"Christian…Do you understand you are going to be a daddy." She asked a little concerned by the lack of words emanating from my mouth. She spoke to me as if I was three year old. I had heard what she had said I just didn't want to believe it and then I panicked.

"I don't want anything to do with you!" I said very sternly and replaced the receiver on its rest. I was gobsmacked to say the least, even numb. Was this really true? I didn't know what confused or saddened me the most. I was gay! I couldn't be a father. I went back to the night we spent together and tried to think of every conceivable way that I could not be the baby's father. I was not part of it all. One night of stupid drunkenness had created a new life. I was brought back to earth with a jolt. She had more or less raped me that night and now she was telling me that I was going to be a father. *"NO! NO! NO! I don't ever want it to be this way!"* I said to myself. If I ever thought about having a baby I would have liked it to happen when I was in a safe and secure relationship. I would have liked to have at least had a say in it and would like to have remembered the event. All I could remember about that night was waking up the next morning in bed beside her totally naked with a mega hangover! This was no way to bring a child into this world.

A baby should be wanted and no alcohol involved, the night should be a romantic night when we just made wonderful and erotic love. Megan! Oh my lord! I hardly knew her!

Three weeks and a day later to that phone call I got another text. *"Gone into labour Please come!"* It saddened me once more and I deleted the message. If I wasn't there I couldn't see it right!? I was not going to live in New York City and I certainly wasn't going to marry her I hardly knew the woman let alone want to spend the rest of my life with her. I definitely wasn't going to move her to Greece so I felt it was best to let the whole thing go and forget about it. Three days later another text came *"Baby girl Sasha five pound three ounces! Congratulations you are a daddy! Megan XXX"* I didn't respond but deleted the message as I had before.

A month later I was being bombarded with texts on a regular basis. I had been paying her for the upkeep of Sasha but she just demanded more and more it was never enough. What the fuck was she doing with my money? Why was she spending it so fast? Was I being made a fool of or what? I made the decision that I never thought I would make. I made immediate reservations for a seat on the next flight to New York. I had to go and sort this out once and for all.

After a quick briefing with Gio and hugs with Luis I headed off to Sport era airport again. It didn't seem real to me…One day I was in Greece the next minute I was in New York. I booked into the hotel I stayed at last time and took a walk through Time Square. I called the number she had left in one of the texts and she answered straight away.

"Christian!" She screamed "Where are you?" She asked.

"I am here, right here in New York Megan. What's your address? I asked her.

"Are you serious? OH MY GOD! Awesome!" She yelled down the phone seeming very excited. She still lived in the same apartment where that fateful night had occurred, so I made my way there. My mind was a little confused as to what I was actually going to say and do once I had got there. My body was a little tired due to the travelling, I wasn't the sort of guy who just sat around I had to get this sorted out. I knocked on the door, Megan opened it.

"Hi Christian! You are looking well." She said

"Thanks.....Erm you are also looking good" Which she did given that she had not long had a baby, her figure was almost back to normal and she did look pretty good. We walked in to the apartment. She took my coat and hung it up in her passage way. She walked a little ahead of me and opened a door, as she pushed it open she said

"Go on Christian, go and say hello to your daughter" I edged into the room and oh my! There on the floor on a pink fluffy rug, lay this tiny little person with the most gorgeous eyes. She was so tiny I stopped in my tracks.

"Oh my god! She's real Megan and she is mine!?" I asked looking at her face.

"Yes she is all yours" She reassured me. I felt a huge warmth run through me. I knelt down beside her and held out my hand. She gripped my finger and was quite content to stare. I had so much to catch up with. My daughter was beautiful, she had hair the same colour as mine and to be honest I really did think she looked like me. I didn't really give two shits for Megan I was not there for her. I could see she had spent her money on furniture and lots of nice things for Sasha. I vowed that minute that Sasha was not going to want for anything ever again; she was going to have the best of everything.

I wasn't going to neglect Luis or Gio and phoned them regularly be it at the house or his work place. I would often tell Luis that I was working, he was too young to understand what was happening, but he knew that when I went to New York that I was working.

The first four days were heaven for me. I got up in the night to feed her and change her. I bathed her and dressed her. I carried her everywhere and didn't mind pushing the stroller. Onlookers must have thought we were a happy couple with a baby. Awe! A nice thought but you would have to be fucking joking! I detested Megan for what she had done and now I had a daughter! She was in her glory with me there. She went to work three nights a week and that saved on a child minder as I was there. She did everything for me, cooking, washing, cleaning and fussed over me as much as she could when I held Sasha. She would do anything she could to be close to me, sometimes I felt as if she was using Sasha to get to me and I felt this was wrong. I was bonding with my little girl Sasha and already she was giving me many smiles and she recognized me, following me with her gaze as I walked around.

Megan began to go out too often now and leaving me to "hold the baby". Don't get me wrong I loved having Sasha and I so wanted to care for her all the time. I just didn't get Megan as a mother! I contacted an old business associate of mine who had done some work for me before and I asked him to follow her on one of her outings. The outcome was astonishing and I paid him very well for an excellent job done.

A few days later I waited for her to get home after her evening out. Sasha was taking a nap. I made Megan a hot coffee and sat in the lounge mellow as could be. She went and changed her shoes and she grabbed her coffee and sat besides me.

"How's baby been?" she asked as she always did.

"Fine" I answered. "Was work good?" I asked her so curious to hear her answer. "Same old shit" she replied.

"What do you do at work again Megan, why don't you tell me" I said looking at her face and not smiling at all. She knew I knew. I stood up fast and pulled out a set of photographs and threw them at her which made her jump.

"You dirty fucking whore" I yelled at her. "You dirty tramp slag!!" I was livid!

"How could you do those things with a baby to look after Megan, you are sick". The photos were of her with men on the floor doing live sex shows.

"I needed the money Christian" She pleaded but I didn't fall for it for a minute

"Err I gave you all the money you asked for Megan" I shouted again

"You are NOT touching Sasha EVER again" I ripped into her.

"How much do you want Megan to stay away from me and Sasha"?

"What?!" she said looking confused.

"Let me have Sasha full time, you can be free to do what you need to do Megan, name your price." It was as easy as that. She named her price, a heavy one too and I agreed.

I was leaving New York City once again and hopefully never to return. I was taking home my daughter all of 4 months old. She was tiny and I loved her. Megan agreed to let me take her home to Greece. I had her passport and permission in writing from Megan to allow me to take her out of the country. I could not believe any mother would sell their child, Megan actually chose the cash.

Once I got Sasha to Greece I knew that Megan would never see her again and I would raise her as well as Luis. There was NO way I was letting a dirty whore like Megan raise my daughter, no way and I swore if anyone tried to take her away from me I would simply kill them.

CHAPTER 20

JEANNE

I had seen his photograph on the internet on one of the gay sites of which there were so many to choose from. His look was of beauty. We began by talking on and off the internet and slowly became friends. He worked long hours so catching him online was difficult at times. So on the opportunities we had to talk we chatted for many hours and shared our news. He had just come out of a long-term relationship and was hesitant to trust again. We had been speaking for many months and had learnt a lot about each other. It was strange but I felt I could open up to him quite freely about my past; which I didn't find too easy to do with most people. We started meeting regularly online and as we got to know each other gradually and feeling more confident we began to webcam too. If you are not PC literate, a webcam is a small camera that links to your computer where you can view the person you are talking to sometimes thousands of miles away. He became quite familiar with Luis and Sasha even before they actually met.

He was six feet four inches tall and built like a "brick shit house". He had huge hands and feet but very beautiful long dark hair which was always beautifully coiffured. He wore earrings in both ears and sported a beard and moustache. If you didn't know he was gay you wouldn't think he was to look at him, not your typical gay looking guy really more your heavy metal rock guy. He appeared to be straight until he spoke to you I guess. He would say things like "hunny" and "sweetheart" a lot. He lived alone in his apartment apart from with his "babies"; they were his cats of which he had 5. He was well mannered and polite spoken with a passion for music of an eclectic taste. It was amazing, after about a year of chatting online he blurted out one night

"I love you Christian!" I was totally amazed. "I always loved you from the very first day. I knew we would get together eventually Christian, what do you say!?" It seemed as if I had chased him for attention for a long time and he finally broke! From day one for me, I was mesmerized by his looks. He was the most beautiful, perfect human being I had ever seen and for me that was perfection! I was not used to imperfections in people and I did not suffer them very well. I knew it meant travelling back to the States but that was ok, as I could always deal with some of the family business whilst I was there. You would have thought that after my happenings with Jay, Kelso and Niko that I wouldn't even bother, but this guy had been through it all with me and he had listened to my fears. Maybe only through the internet or phone but all the same he felt my pain.

It was absolutely fucking piss hilarious when we had our first phone call!! I couldn't understand him very much. I had been around Yankees before but his accent was different to those in the North and a lot faster! He couldn't understand me either which was hardly surprising as the language which I spoke was a mixture of Greek and English with a bit of an American twang as I was being taught by Americans in New York, English in UK, but predominantly Greek when I was in Corfu so I just thrashed my way through the conversation and did the best I could and hoped and prayed we would understand each other somehow. The call went on for a while causing many many laughs and I learnt as we went along. My accent was some way between Greek and French which I guess made me a Grench or a Freek (I know what some would say!). The more we phoned each other and the more we spoke the easier it became and we began understanding each other. We talked about all sorts of things, everything and nothing really each of us hanging on to the others words and as the days went by we spoke more often than not. Sometimes five times a day we would speak and then again during the endless hours through the night. We would play music to each other and I would attempt to sing to him although I couldn't sing a note and was tone deaf! We laughed so much we spent many hours sharing tears too.

I was living back in Greece and now I found myself again holidaying in mid Central America. Phone calls and cam sessions were not enough anymore so I took up Jeanne's offer and travelled over to stay with him. We had already shared so much and were so in love and felt that nothing could ever go wrong!

He would be there to meet us when we landed and got off the plane. He brought his truck as I had quite a bit of luggage with me. I was in my denims and white shirt shades on top of my head pushing Sasha in the Barbie stroller with Luis walking along side holding on. They were very tired from all the travelling we had done but were in reasonable spirits as they were also excited about seeing Jeanne. I spotted Jeanne and he was almost jumping up and down on the spot! Tears fell from his eyes with excitement and laughter. He was even more beautiful in the flesh. My God! How perfect he was and he was all mine. He looked right into my eyes as I took my shades off the top of my head and we smiled the smile of two people in love.

"Hi! Christian! At long last!!!!!" He said kissing me on both cheeks.

"Well hello to you too!" I said as we chuckled in total disbelief that we had at last met!

"This is Luis" I said pointing in Luis' direction and sitting as a lady of leisure is Sasha modelling a beautiful Barbie stroller!" We both laughed as this was our sort of humour and it felt as if we had known each other all our lives.

"They loved the airplane flight!" I said this seemed to break the ice and we all began guffawing with laughter and talking as much and as fast as we ever did on the phone. Luis jumped in with questions every now and then. We talked all the way to Jeanne's pad and by the end of the journey we all felt as if this was meant to be, it seemed so natural. I was pleased and Jeanne looked as if he was in his glory.

His apartment was snug and cosy and he kept it very clean. The kids were happy to meet the man they had got to know over the phone and internet. We looked at each other and smiled a lot and then just stared and stared each not wanting to loose the others gaze. That first night was heaven come true. The kids had crashed within an hour of arriving so this then gave Jeanne and I some long awaited alone time. We carried them into Jeanne's bedroom and laid them on his queen size water bed. They were out like lights and looked so content. Jeanne had waited so long to hug and kiss them and tuck them into bed. He got a little emotional at times but he was doing well. Now we were alone for the very first time.

"Is it ok if I smoke please Jeanne?" I asked with the utmost respect.

"Yeah!!! Sure you can" He replied just still not taking his eyes off me and offering me a cigarette from his beautiful gold monogrammed cigarette case. He had style that was for sure. He held out a lighter to light my cigarette and our hands touched.... The electricity was amazing and it sent small electric shocks all through my body letting my body take control of me. My heart beat heavily, I puffed on the cigarette and smoked it whilst looking into his beautiful eyes, just looking and smiling. This passion was wild! He leant forward and put his hand gently on my face and touched my lips. I stuck out my tongue which made him put his hand round the back of my neck and pulled me into him and we kissed. *BANG – PERZAZZ – WHOO HOO _ KER-CHING!!!!!!!!!!!* It was almost like fireworks going off. We fit so well together and it was natural too such a beautiful gentle man he was and oh so loving and giving. He wanted to adopt the kids as his own too. He so adored Luis and Sasha and they in turn seemed to have trusted him from the off, I suppose kids have a sixth sense about people sometimes. We looked for a joint business venture that we could grow together. I had enough funds to start the business and we were both going to work hard at it. Obviously my interest lay in dance schools and I had thoughts of owning a chain of them one day.

The holiday would be over soon and it was all too much to bear. We couldn't separate now – we were a family and we were happy. Who said we couldn't have two homes anyway. Paradisia would always be mine and my dance business was doing really well.

We found the perfect building! It was to be a combined dance studio/beauty salon. I would teach the dance and he would do the hair. It was the perfect business for us so we bought it. We had to move to another part of the States but that didn't matter, we were going somewhere fresh and the weather was extremely acceptable. He didn't like my private work, you know, the family business. He begged me on many occasions to let it go. All I could honestly promise him was that I wouldn't cage fight anymore. I really wasn't prepared to do the fighting anymore, I had people to do that and I still earned a few bucks at managing them. He liked the big house and the salon/studio, he liked the Harleys parked in the driveway. The closet was full of clothes I bought him and the boots and shoes to complete the outfits too. He liked the lifestyle and wanted it as much as I craved it. We could have survived handsomely on Niko's left over estate and the new business, but I couldn't just let it go like that, I had my reputation and honour to defend.

I missed home a lot; the sand here wasn't quite the same as back home under your feet. I guess I tried so hard to mould the new house to be another "Paradisia". I put in marble flooring everywhere and had all the rooms painted creams and whites. I even had a few palm trees in the front drive, but even though I tried very hard, it was not home and never would be. The people were nice and the weather was glorious but still I pined for home.

I buried myself in my work teaching dancing six days a week. I had to keep busy, work lots and think little. I tried so hard to be the husband that Jeanne deserved and wanted me to be. I wanted to please him so much but I couldn't just cut out my family business and the people in my life. More to the point I didn't want to let it all go. I had grown up with all this in my life I wasn't going to stop now. I couldn't let it go and Jeanne often said to let NIKO go! I never said anything to those comments but just listened and I knew that deep down he could very well be right.

CHAPTER 21

JESEE

_____

Jeanne and I had the house set up pretty well and we furnished it how we wanted. I had tried to make this house similar to Paradisia in a way; it was painted all in cream and white throughout the house and dressed the rooms with elaborate materials, giving a touch of opulence to the home. The salon/studio was doing pretty well; profits were up as were the clientele. We had new enquiries everyday and most of them became members.

Jeanne would often take the "MOM" role in the relationship and therefore spent a lot of time with Luis and Sasha. I preferred it this way it made life easy for me. He loved being in the kitchen with a ""pinnie"" on and to be honest he was a dab hand in the cooking department. If I didn't work out as much as I did I would be getting quite large by now. Jeanne would take the kids on the school run which he thoroughly enjoyed and would be the first to see them come running out of school with their entire make and do projects they would bring home at the end of the day. In fact he did practically all the things that needed doing and therefore the time we spent together was precious. Having children in the house a quiet peaceful ambience would be shattered as soon as they walked through the front door. We needed to travel at time too so we arranged for a nanny to look after the children so that Jeanne and I could do what we needed to with no worry about the children. This person was going to have to be pretty special to take care of my daughter and my brother. Thinking of being in this situation sent my mind wandering back to the time I was with Gio, he was the best with the children; he had a heart which only they understood. After what that bastard did you would think I wouldn't have any fond memories, but there are a few.

We found Jesee through word of mouth. Other mums at the school told of how she had always been minding children, I asked Louise for her number when she brought her son round for a play date with Luis. I gave her a call.

"Hi! Is this Jesee?" I asked

"Yes!" Who am I speaking to?" Was the reply from the other end?

"My name is Christian and I was given your number by Louise from the Pre School. She tells me you are an excellent childminder." I said introducing myself.

"Ah! Yes!" She replied and followed "I have heard of you! How can I help you?"

"OK! I have two children and my partner and I need to travel for our business. Would you be interested in coming to see me and have a chat about maybe you working for us and taking care of our children? I have it on good authority that you are an excellent minder" Hoping that she understood my accent I awaited a response.

"Wow! Yes I would be very interested. When would you like me to come?"

"If you could come tomorrow morning say around ten thirty? Would that be ok for you?" I asked.

"Yes! Yes! That would be great! Many thanks. I look forward to meeting you tomorrow at ten thirty. I will get a cab over to you please could you give me your address?"

"Its ok I have your address I will send a car for you. I look forward to meeting you. Many thanks" I said as I replaced the receiver in its cradle.

Ten thirty arrived and Jeanne was sitting in the lounge waiting for the arrival of Jesee. I hope she was punctual I thought, I could not bear lateness and impoliteness. Her first impression would certainly be all I would need to assess her suitability for what I wanted.

The doorbell rang and Tylor (the butler) answered the door.

"How can I help you?" He would say in his authoritative way. A more loyal butler you couldn't find.

"Hi! My name is Jesee and Mr Miyarou asked me to come for an interview for a nanny position at 10.30 this morning. Would it be possible to see him please?" She asked. It sounded as if she was quite astounded at the house. Tylor bade her enter the foyer where she waited with patience until I was ready for her. I actually stood at the top of the stirs and looked down into the foyer to see what she was doing. I could see her pacing the floor catching herself in a mirror as she walked up and down the foyer waiting. She was very patient as I made her wait for 20 minutes longer than I had asked her to be there. I was testing her mettle and she had passed.

Tylor opened the door and stood proud against it announcing the arrival of Jesee.

"Miss Jesee Glade. Sir!"

"Thankyou Tylor you may leave us" Jeanne said as he left the room and I joined them and offered to take Jesee's jacket. I could see she had taste in clothes and was a bright vivacious young girl. She didn't look old enough to have done as much child minding as she had, but all her clients were very praiseworthy of her and spoke very highly of her.

Please take a seat." I offered. I didn't want her standing through the whole process. I sat one side of the desk with Jeanne and Jesee sat opposite. She seemed pretty impressed with the house and for that I was glad. It would make life a lot easier for her is she liked where she would be working.

"Thankyou Mr Miyarou" She uttered.

"Hey! Let's get off on a good foot shall we? Firstly NEVER call me Mr Miyarou! That is THE most important thing. My name is Christian. Most people call me Chris." She blushed a little having no idea what she would be getting into.

She was eighteen. A mature eighteen year old, and she had three years experience of babysitting and child minding children from a few months old to ten years old. She was training to be a qualified nursery nurse. Jeanne and I wanted to meet her but the final decision would be Jeanne's as he was in the house more than I was as I worked long hours and with all sorts of business dealing popping up I had to be away a lot. She came to the house whilst the children were elsewhere. She was young looking with long dark hair and she was very beautiful with soft brown eyes. I know I am gay but she was a breath of fresh air and she seemed to light up the room when she walked in. With her looks and her body she could have been a top model or a show girl or something, but she seemed a bit head strong about her career and what she wanted to achieve. She wasn't fazed at all when she realised we were a family of two dads and no mum. The interview went well and both Jeanne and I took to her and felt the children would be happy with her too. She was hired!

Jesse's job was to be there in the morning to supervise Luis and Sasha in their task of getting ready for school. Once they were ready she would take them to school and nursery. At the end of the school day Jesse would be there to pick them up and take them home, Sasha finished at 12.30 as she was at nursery and Luis would be picked up at 3.30pm.

Jesse didn't have to cook as we had other staff that did the everyday chores of cooking and cleaning etc. Jeanne liked to cook so mostly he cooked for everyone; he thought he was a Marco Pierre White in the kitchen and that he deserved a few Michelin stars for his cooking. Jeanne didn't like people in HIS kitchen as he put it. Jess would then look after the children until bed time and then put them to bed. She would read them a story to help them go to sleep. Sometimes I would look through the gap in the door and just watch her with them. They seemed very happy and it was a joy to see the children happy for a change. A routine was what we needed for our home as then everyone knew where they were and what they had to do. She got to know her way around the house pretty quickly and had settled in well. She had her own phone and computer in her room and an endless supply of food and drink whenever she wanted it. She had weekends off unless we wanted to go somewhere, and she didn't mind working then as for her it meant double pay, so she never said no! Most importantly the children had taken to her very well and I liked having her around the house but Jeanne held back on his true feelings. I would watch him sometimes looking at her and then throw his head back and when he thought nobody was looking would make a chuff sound to show he wasn't that enamoured with her. I didn't think she was the brightest spark in the toolbox but she did her job and the children adored her, personally I think Jeanne was a little jealous of her beauty, however she was sweet and her innocence played well. I could relate to her youthful energy and the mistakes that she made but I always consoled her and pointed her in the right direction if she needed help. Her grandmother was Greek but originated from a different island from Corfu where I was born. Her grandfather was an American – hence why she was born and raised in the States. She knew little Greek and not much more of her family's history on the Greek island where her grandmother came from. Sometimes I would take the time to sit and converse with her, we would spend a lot of time together walking in the garden, sitting by the pool and many other places where we could spend time alone so that I could tell her all about home, where her ancestors came from and the lives they all lead. I taught her Greek words too and sometimes we would try and have a conversation in Greek. She was a quick learner I have to say and it wasn't long before we were chatting away like we had known each other all our lives, the evidence of our closeness became noticeable when Jeanne was around, I think he felt a bit left out when we rambled on in Greek. The crunch came on a day when as soon as I arose from my sleep you could cut the atmosphere with a knife. I got the impression something big was about to happen.

"You are spending TOO much time with the staff Christian" Jeanne blurted this out when you would have least expected him too. We were having a quiet evening in, I thought it was so we could spend some quality time together, how wrong I was, I began to think that the whole day had been contrived and that he knew exactly what he was doing. He was a very jealous man and I felt sometimes that he thought of me as HIS property. He liked nobody around me and I guess I had not been aware of how much Jesee made me smile when she was around. He obviously had noticed. Funny how we are not aware of how our body language can be read and how much effect other peoples actions ours may have. I didn't treat Jesee as staff she was more than that to me. We talked, laughed and spent time with the children together. It was almost as if we were a family, just the 4 of us. It was fast becoming obvious to Jeanne that Jesee and I were getting a bit too close for his comfort. There had to be an element of closeness with a nanny when they are looking after your children you have to be sure that they are going to be well cared for. These feelings took me back to when I was a boy. A question I had often been asked was "How do you know you are gay if you have never tried a woman?" That was a confusing time for me and I had these same feelings again when Jess was around. We would be close some days and swim days were heavenly! We would lie around the pool for hours; in fact I would go as far as to say that I spent more time with Jess than I did Jeanne. She was beautiful to look at whenever you looked at her. She was perfect even in her sleep. Yes! I did used to peek in the door and look at her lying in bed with the moonlight streaking across her face and lighting her up like an angel. Her long black hair stretched out across her white pillow. Out by the pool she would strut around so elegantly her hair swept over her shoulders and her body glistening in the sunlight. A vision....There is no other way to describe her. One night Jeanne had told me off

"You should NOT be swimming together!!! You guys look like an item!!!!" He screamed at me his face reddening up as it always did when he started to lose it!

"The whole place is talking about you AND YOUR TART! Christian! Don't you know that!!!!! Don't you hear what they are saying? Or don't you care?" He was spitting razor blades with every word that came out of his mouth. Now it was my turn!

"I don't give a TOSS what the locals think Jeanne! They can go to hell! WHOEVER doesn't like it can GO TO HELL!!!!!!!!!!!!" And I stormed out of the room slamming the door on my way so hard that the wall shook. He had pissed me off so much I really didn't even want to look at him anymore. I guess after how Niko had been with me and forbade me to do so many things I was NOT going to listen to Jeanne and jealous rantings of a ponced up queen. I didn't want to be told what to do ever again.

The rantings of Jeanne that night had the opposite effect of what he had hoped. It didn't stop me seeing Jess and infact we probably went overboard as she often sat on my lap around the lounge and the poolside and we would hug and talk and laugh A LOT! We would confide in each other too, telling each other secrets we wouldn't normally share with anyone. But she was so easy to talk to and I was having feelings that I never knew existed and I liked them. I had never been this close to a woman before; maybe I was wrong maybe it is good with a woman.

One morning after dropping the kids off at school and nursery I decided to take Jess shopping. She wasn't a greedy girl and was kind of shy when we began shopping as she had never had this done for her before and she was pretty loathe to accept my gifts to her, but she mellowed and was having as much fun shopping as I did. I must have spent a small fortune on her. She had new jeans, tops, shoes and sandals, a few dresses, new bag, makeup and toiletries too. With a smile and a kiss she always thanked me. I loved spoiling her and she looked so happy just like a child in a sweetie shop.

"You will have to model them for me later" I said jokingly at the shop counter. Both Jess and the shopkeeper blushed and jess's little cheeks went so red she looked a little like Snow White from the fairytale. We made our way out of the Mall to the car and then on to our home for some light refreshment and maybe a swim. I can tell you I was really looking forward to the fashion show I was about to get too.

We arrived home and I saw Jeanne's car in the driveway, we sat for a few minutes and looked at each other, we both breathed a bit of a sigh and opened the car knowing what was going to happen. We opened the trunk of the car and took out our spoils. As soon as we stepped through the front door there he was. OH MY GOD!!!!!! He looked absolutely livid. Typical position for giving a telling off and for a split second I felt almost as if I was back at home with Mama and her telling me off when I had been out late and got into mischief. He stood there feet apart back straight and arms folded across his chest. His face looked contorted inside I was laughing he looked like an angry Genie just let out of a bottle. It was quite amusing to see and I chuckled to myself, looked at Jess and offered her to go upstairs and sort things out. She looked at me a little worried but I motioned that all would be well.

We ventured into the lounge where Jeanne erupted like Mount Vesuvius. A torrent of anger, jealousy and abuse emanated from his mouth like a dragon breathing fire.

"I AM ABOUT SICK OF HEARING GOSSIP ABOUT YOU TWO! Get a grip Christian YOU ARE GAY and you ARE MINE!!!!!!!! Yes! MY husband remember!"

"GOD HOW COULD I FORGET!" I shouted back and stormed out myself. I wasn't going to suffer anymore of his verbal abuse and jealousy. This had to stop!

One evening quite early, Jess had put the children to bed and came down and made herself a cup of tea.

"I appreciate everything you do for me Jess, you know that don't you?" I said as she handed me the cup she had just made me.

Jeanne had gone to bed early and I just wasn't tired so I was relaxing while Jess had gotten the kids ready for bed and now we could both relax. I rolled a spliff and kicked back on the sofa.

"Come here – sit by me Jess" I motioned to her as she began to sit on a chair opposite. She moved and came to sit next to me and we were shoulder to shoulder.

"Jess" I said quietly looking into her eyes "You are so very beautiful you know" I lifted my arm and stroked her hair. She wasn't shy of me she was just quite innocent and that so appealed to me. I looked at her eyes the smouldering dark eyes which said so many things to me.

"Jess – I need to…" and then BANG! I kissed her full on the mouth and she kissed me back. The kiss lingered for what seemed a life time and so very passionate our tongues feeling for each other. She was not a loud mouth in your face Saskia nor was she take what you want Megan. She was so very mystical and different. Our kisses were getting more passionate and we clung to each other feeling each others bodies. Her breasts heaving with want for me. We rolled to the floor and our feelings ran away with us. I felt her wanting me as much as I wanted her.

Her blouse fell open revealing her beautiful soft skin I started to explore her. Lifting my head at intervals to take in the gorgeous expressions of enjoyment on her face made me want her more, I caught a glimpse of her looking at me too a smile shone from her lips as she whispered how much she wanted me. She was shining just like an angel. I sat astride her and gently peeled off each layer of clothing. I kissed her mouth, her eyes, and her forehead. Wandering slowly down to her neck, so beautiful and long, I moved to her ears and sucked on her lobes, this drove her wild with passion. She lay back almost exhausted her arms up over her head as if she was giving herself to me. My manhood was throbbing with want. I removed myself and took off my clothes. I knelt down beside her, every move I made she followed with those haunting eyes of hers. I began to remove her jeans. I knelt at her feet and ran my hands up her legs and kissing her belly, a gasp and a sigh emulated from her. Each one making me want her more. I undid the button and zipper on her jeans and gently but firmly pulled them down and followed them with my tongue up and down her legs. She lifted herself as if for me to kiss her pussy, but I wasn't going there yet. This was new to me and I wanted to enjoy every minute. I grabbed her jeans by the ankles and removed them from her. I separated her legs gently and lay between them. I had come this far and it was out of this world but was I ready to go the whole way? Just a tiny doubt flickered in the back of my brain "You are gay! You don't go with women!" I ignored this thought and slowly but firmly started to make love with her. This was UNBELIEVABLE. I pushed a little bit more and finally all the way in. We lay there for a little joined together and began to kiss each other once more. It was so good being inside a woman. I could feel her pulsating, I moved myself in and out of her each time getting a little more urgent. I pushed and pushed for all I was worth, the noises she was making were making me want her more. Jeanne was asleep upstairs and I really didn't want to wake him right now. I gently put my fingers to her lips. She tried to keep her enjoyment to a dull moaning. We fucked as if it was our last time together hard and fast it went on for quite a few minutes, I held on for as long as I could and could contain myself no more. We orgasmed at the same time and it was magnifico!!!!!!! We fell in a heap I went just to the side of her and we just lay in each others arms, our bodies soaked with the sweat of our lovemaking. Maybe I was bi sexual now not just gay. HHmmmmmm I had to think about this one. This was a big thing for me I hadn't realised that I could make love to a woman. We laid and rested our hearts beating fast and just holding each other and we fell asleep.

That morning came as a shock for all of us. I awoke to find Jesee in my arms on the lounge floor both of us naked. She looked so peaceful sleeping. I looked around the room. My God! It was 8am already; we must have fallen asleep about 5am. There was a letter on the coffee table addressed to me.

TO MY HUSBAND –I decided not to wake you and your tart. I hope you have a nice life together. I have said my goodbyes to the kids. You will be fine, they love Jesee to pieces. Despite everything I wish you only happiness. I loved you. Jeanne

He had left me. I went upstairs to check our room and sure enough he had removed every bit of clothing he owned, along with cases to put them in. I sat on the edge of the bed and tried to take it all in. Jesee walked through my bedroom door with Sasha on her hip and holding Luis' hand. I kissed the kids good morning and told them that school was cancelled for today.

"We are going to have a fun pool day instead" I sad and they all jumped for joy. They loved the times we spent together as family.

I knew as the week progressed that I would soon have to return home. Yes back to Greece! Jeanne and I had discussed our finances and I was going to sell my half of the business and he could keep the house. The paperwork didn't take long to finalise and within a month I was taking my family home to Greece with an addition.

FAREWELL AMERICA!

CHAPTER 22

LIFE UPDATED

So! There you have it......20+ years of an amazing life so far and it goes on BUT that is another story.

I have travelled far, to all sorts of countries and different places but note I always ended back here at Paradisia. Now home to my wife Jesee, my brother Luis and my daughter Sasha.

To this day I am still afraid of the dark; it brings to mind Niko's eyes watching me ready to pounce on me, the defenceless prey

Paradisia's name was changed to "Destiny" and we had a new house sign made and put up. A lot of the décor and furniture have changed and it has become more of a home than before, with love and laughter and warmth. It's been a long journey so far but with so much further to go to experience. Life, I have found can be so short lived. I am still very youthful and still remain very vain. I work out everyday in my studio and I teach dance as and when I want to. The studio is doing really well and has built up a good clientele and a great deal of respect. We have a solid staff of eleven and the place is rocking and thriving. Everyone is good at what they do.

Dance work is extremely busy and the studio has built up a good reputation. I got so busy teaching and I was feeling it for the first time, now there was tons of paperwork, scheduling and payroll. The studio had taken off and I held a sense of achievement when I would see my students pass their exams and put on shows at least once a year. I have the best highly trained tutors and a studio with all amenities including a licensed bar. The tuition which we offer is of a very high quality and is open to all types of dance and people. We have:- Ballroom, Latin American, Disco, Rock and Roll, Mambo, Salsa, American Line Dancing, Street Dance and of course traditional Greek dancing with personalized dancers for your special day

Now I am a giant in stature and strength with a victory over Niko the world is there for me to take.

Jesee and I had a traditional Greek wedding. Many people stared at my wife when she was on my arm *"She's the girl who turned Christians head!"* they would gossip!!!! My business clients joked

"Young girl right for breeding and all that" They would say. They were fine ones to talk they all had wives and mistresses and some even had boyfriends, so from where I was standing it was a bit like the pot calling the kettle black. I was content with my wife and family. She had become Mummy to Sasha and she and Luis got on very well. Jess struggled sometimes; I mean a big house, two children and me to contend with along with all the hustle and bustle that my business brought to the house. It was lot for a young naïve nineteen year old girl to deal with. She liked nice things though and it wasn't before long that she liked the best things.

I have come a long way since first having a dance studio and all these responsibilities I often thought of those who had been and gone such as Gio and Saskia and thinking about the night of the beach party. It made me think back.

This would mean the big barbecue would come out and the alcohol would flow, everyone would chill in swimwear feeling free. We always had gatherings like this it gave a bit of a family feel. They occurred on a regular basis and Gio and I decided to take Sasha with us on this particular night.

We told Saskia bring Luis to join us. As always Luis had a big smile on his face when he saw us and ran with his arms outstretched towards us. Saskia, as always; looked shitfaced and headed straight for the free drinks. I made the decision then to take Luis home that night as she would be in no fit state to care for him. We stayed for about two hours; we ate and had a little to drink. The kids were spoilt by everyone and they were fussed over in a big way. Sasha crashed out in her stroller all covered up in her baby "blankie" and Luis began yawning so we took that as the cue to go home. Luis climbed up into my arms and snuggled up to my chest, as I held him tight to me I said

"I will always be there for you Luis ALWAYS" and stroked his face. I was watching as Saskia was throwing herself at all sorts of guys.

"Gio! Do me a favour please get Sasha in the car" and gave him a look only he knew. I was watching as Gio put Sasha in the car along with Luis, both settled in their car seats.

"Goodbye Saskia!" I whispered and I turned to get in the car. I glimpsed one last time at the beach and saw Saskia and the guys entering the sea for a swim before I drove off.

We arrived home and put the children to bed then relaxed on the sofa and cuddled up with a spliff to finish the night off. We were just starting to really relax and fall asleep and my mobile rang. It was Den from the bar....

"Christian, I am sorry but we can't find Saskia is she at your place?"

"No!" I said "When was the last time you saw her?"

"Well she went towards the sea a while ago, everyone else has returned but not her!" He said sounding rather anxious.

"I shouldn't worry about it Den she will have passed out somewhere with someone as usual. Don't worry about it she will turn up when she wants some more drugs!!!" I said sarcastically. Well after all that was what she was all about now, just getting drugs in her. Niko really had done a number on her. I felt sorry for her in a way but she could have developed some back bone and got herself sorted. Now I didn't give a damn about her! She had done this too many times and I was not going to let her ruin our precious times.

Many days and nights passed, and there was still no sign of Saskia. Nobody had heard from her or seen her since the night of the party and she went walking along the beach with the guys who couldn't resist her when she was high. The emergency services were called but nobody knew anything and it was as if she had just disappeared of the face of the earth. She was never heard of again! Sometime later the legalities came into action and an inquest was arranged. At court the verdict was *"Death by drowning under the influence of alcohol and a class 2 substance.*

Accidental" Luis would be fine; he couldn't miss what had never been there in the first place.

I worked the family business from home mostly. I made plenty of changes. I stopped the protection collecting and I also warned off the other collectors. I had made the decision I wasn't going to take any hard earned money off someone just for the sake of it. As a result of this decision, people began to respect me, they had thought I would become like Niko, but I wanted to be the COMPLETE opposite to him. A few meetings were held in restaurants and the top pins were apologetic to my past experience with Niko. I just plodded through it with the determination that I was not going to become a mean bastard like Niko. They knew I wasn't a mug, I was known to have a short fuse and I liked the best of everything. I had employed a chauffeur, a gardener, a house cleaner and a pool boy. Oh yes! Everyone of any stature had to have a pool boy. I got involved in whatever the gardener was doing as I loved my back yard. The garden was too huge to deal with by myself so I had to find someone I could get on with and who had the same ideas as me. The chauffeur took Luis to school every day and picked him up. He also took Jesee where she wanted to go. The house cleaner was employed as Jesee didn't like housework or have the time to clean. Anyway, why have all this money and not use it to make our lives a bit easier. She liked to spend money though! Oh yes, she would think nothing of going and buying as many pairs of shoes as she could fit in her wardrobe. You think Imelda Marcos was bad! My God!!! She was 10 times worse. I am surprised there are any shoes left in the shops. Her friends would visit on a regular basis and would completely take over the house. I didn't like this. It was MY house not hers. They only wanted her for what they could get out of her; they weren't real friends' just spongers who would bleed her and ultimately ME! To whatever they could get. I hated them and told her not to let them come round anymore, but her in her infinite wisdom let them take her for the biggest ride.

Sasha was my doll. She was unique and beautiful in every way and she held the chords on my heart strings. No matter what happened during the day all I had to do was look at her or think about her and I would smile. She truly was my daughter one I thought I would never have. Well let's face it...How many poofs have kids! She melted my heart and I could deny her nothing. Sasha was a Daddies girl and I wanted her above anyone else.

When Jesee got pregnant I worried a little as she didn't appear to be the most doting of women. You could usually tell if someone was as they say "maternal" and Jesee certainly wasn't. She oozed beauty though, it was true women really did glow when they were pregnant. Sasha wanted a sister and Luis wanted a brother. We built a nursery together and chose whites, creams and yellows to decorate it. As always Jesee chose the best of everything and I footed the bill, but we had to buy other gifts too, Sasha and Luis could not miss out. I thought to myself just how lucky we were to be in this new position we had found ourselves in, plenty of money so there were no financial worries and the best of everything. I had sold my business in the States and received a good deal of money for it. Enough to make us more secure anyway. It was at times like this when I would think of Mama and how she tried to give me the best of everything, but all I wanted was her. She was everything to me. How things had changed how different it all was now! I didn't attend her funeral and I didn't regret it either. She had taken me on when I was two years of age. My birth mother had been a French dancer called Riana. She danced in the gentlemen's clubs and that was where Niko had met her all those years ago, funny how that is where he met ME also! She died of a drugs overdose when she was twenty two years old. Niko apparently went to pieces after her death and couldn't take care of me anymore so he handed me over to a local Greek family headed by Mama and Toni. I always knew he wasn't my father but Mama! I ALWAYS believed Mama was my mother and that is why I was so devastated when the truth came out. I could not forgive her for lying to me all my life.

"Mama! Why didn't you tell me? I loved and worshipped the floor you once walked upon. Now you are gone and it's too late." I often said these words but no amount of stewing on them was going to change anything.

Everyone once dear to me had either died or disappeared. Gio got too close... he had a good head for numbers and could speak really well, so I hired him for a short time to be my personal assistant, but one day I caught him taking money from the safe without permission, not just once either. Once I could forgive but persistent theft and above all lying was not my cup of tea. I became hardened to people disappearing.

People came people went, THAT was my life!

EPILOG

Jesee had insisted on a home birth and even though the professionals advised her that with having her first baby it should really be in a hospital, but she would not have it; Jess had her way, as always.

The labour was quite heavy and long drawn and she took hours to deliver. I stayed with her through out it all and it took me back to when Luis was born, sentimental feelings.

At 3.15am my son was born.

A son, my first son!!!!! A sense of pride oozed out of me as I put my arms out to take a hold of him as they handed him to me. He was super tiny weighing 4 pound and 2 ounces.

Jesee had done fine. She did well and I had to look after her now.

My son, he looked so beautiful.

His name …. Niki!

LOOK OUT FOR
THE SEQUAL

Authoress & Editor